WHISTLING PAST THE GRAVEYARD

Prequel to The Saga of Shadows

WHISTLING PAST THE GRAVEYARD

Prequel to The Saga of Shadows

New York Times bestselling author

KEVIN J. ANDERSON

WordFire Press
Colorado Springs, Colorado

ISBN: 978-1-61475-490-9

Cover design by Janet McDonald

Cover art by Stephen Youll

Kevin J. Anderson, Art Director

Book Design by RuneWright, LLC
www.RuneWright.com

Published by
WordFire Press, an imprint of
WordFire, Inc.
PO Box 1840
Monument CO 80132

Kevin J. Anderson & Rebecca Moesta, Publishers

WordFire Press Trade Paperback Edition September 2016
Printed in the USA
wordfirepress.com

CHAPTER ONE

Rlinda Kett

As she flew the *Voracious Curiosity* in a sparse sector of the Spiral Arm, Rlinda Kett discovered Happiness. Or rediscovered it, more correctly.

According to Confederation records, no one had received word from the isolated colony since the end of the destructive Elemental War. The planet Happiness had been settled by hardy and ambitious neo-Amish families with no interest in galactic politics. They just wanted to be left alone.

Back in the days of the Terran Hanseatic League, when Chairman Basil Wenceslas opened up many new unsettled worlds connected by the network of Klikiss transportals—alien dimensional gateways that allowed instantaneous travel from point to point—the neo-Amish had signed up for the colonization initiative. They'd taken their group of four hundred followers through the trapezoidal stone doorways, claiming the isolated world for their own.

No one had heard from them in more than nine years.

Flying alone aboard her comfortable old ship, Rlinda relaxed in the cockpit as she watched the mottled, blue-green sphere grow larger. Ever since the unexpected death of her beloved Branson Roberts, "BeBob," she had not chosen a new copilot. She calculated her course by herself and arrowed the *Curiosity* in, ready to find her place in orbit.

Because Rlinda was such a large woman, she had made a special expansion modification to the pilot's seat. She had dark skin, a big booming laugh, and a warm personality that put everyone at ease. For several years now she had served as the Confederation's Trade Minister, because King Peter had specifically asked her to fill that role. Despite that, she was more proud of her cooking skills and the restaurants she owned and managed.

Now, as she flew toward the isolated planet, hoping to reestablish contact with the colony, she lounged back to eat a late lunch: savory glazed vegetables enhanced with minced medusa frills, a recipe of her own devising, which she featured on the main menu of all her restaurants. Rlinda never skimped on her preparations in the galley, even if it was just for herself, as much as if she were with a large group of friends.

After dabbing her lips with a napkin, she activated the comm. "Hello, Happiness. This is Rlinda Kett from the Confederation, reestablishing contact. Can anybody hear me down there?"

Since her arrival was a surprise, she didn't expect an instant answer. Scanning ahead, she detected no other space traffic, no ships in orbit, no obvious cities on the planetary surface. The neo-Amish had colonized Happiness only a dozen years ago, and given their general avoidance of advanced technology, she didn't exactly expect the few hundred of them to build a gigantic metropolis in that amount of time.

After five minutes of silence, she clicked the comm again. "Anytime you want to respond."

She finished her meal, set the plate aside, and reached forward to pick up the small silver capsule on the piloting console. She rolled it between her thumb and forefinger, wearing a bittersweet smile.

"I told you we'd go interesting places together, BeBob. I always liked traveling with you, though I preferred doing it when you were alive." She touched her lips to the capsule of his compacted ashes and set it back on the console. "You're still my favorite ex-husband." She heaved a long sigh, but decided not to ruin her day. Instead, she savored the lingering taste and pondered what she might have for dessert.

After another five minutes of silence she picked up her dishes, cycled them through the sanitizer, then returned to the pilot's chair. Since the neo-Amish weren't talkative, she decided to search a little harder for them.

She activated the *Curiosity*'s sensor suite and scanned across all communication bands, but detected no activity. Next, she flew over planet's the night side, but found no city lights in the darkness. Orbiting back into daylight, she ran a more rigorous inspection of the primary continent. She tracked down some weathered old alien ruins, crumbling cities abandoned by the insect race—likely the location of the transportal wall. When the hardy colonists had come through the dimensional gateway, taking a chance on this new and unexplored world, they would have built their own settlements nearby.

But so much had happened since then. The Elemental War grew more destructive; the nearly invincible alien combatants destroyed countless populations, and then the long-vanished Klikiss race returned to reclaim their former planets. Many fledgling settlements, like Happiness, were wiped out.

She still received no response from the colony below.

"Hello down there?" she said aloud. "I hope you're not waiting for somebody to come and help …"

In the nine years since the end of the War, the Spiral Arm had engaged in a full-scale recovery operation, reconnecting lost colonies. King Peter and Queen Estarra strengthened the Confederation from the jungle world of Theroc, remaking human government into a unified and supportive power structure, rather than the oppressive Terran Hanseatic League that had been ruled by the iron-fisted Chairman Wenceslas.

At the end of the War, the powerful elemental beings had seemed defeated, but what if the capricious sentient fireballs, the faeros, or the destructive and vengeful liquid-crystal hydrogues had come back to destroy isolated colonies like Happiness? Or what if the innocent, helpless neo-Amish were obliterated in the Klikiss invasion to reclaim their old worlds? Would anyone have known?

She pressed the comm again. "You all are making me very nervous up here. Anybody listening?"

As the Confederation's Trade Minister, Rlinda had important duties, but she also liked to fly her ship and explore. Now that the Confederation was stable, she felt it was time to search out those worlds that had fallen through the cracks. Some of those misplaced colonies had indeed been found. A few were thriving, a few needed help, and a few had been destroyed. She didn't know which category Happiness would fall under.

She continued to scan for any indications of a power grid or a newly built city—hell, she would even settle for a small town. Her heart grew heavy as she decided she might have to cross this colony off the list.

Then, she did discover two small settlements not far from the broken and moss-covered Klikiss ruins. Rectangular patches of crops stood out against the otherwise untouched natural vegetation. The main town and the farmlands were nestled in a broad, gentle valley near the abandoned ruins, while a second, smaller village was higher up in the hills and tiny dots of what must be livestock.

Hope blossomed inside her. As she descended through the calm atmosphere, angling toward the larger settlement in the valley, Rlinda picked up BeBob's ashes again. "I prefer a happy ending to the story. Let's go down and say hello."

Rlinda was the gregarious one, while BeBob would have been a loner if she hadn't constantly dragged him out of his shell. He'd been a skinny man with frizzy gray hair and a nervous disposition, and she had adored him. They had experienced so many adventures together, had such a wild and exciting romance, and they had wanted to retire together when it was all over. It had been so perfect; their very own happy ending.

Rlinda wrapped her fingers around the capsule of his ashes as tears welled in her large brown eyes. Then one day, BeBob had dropped dead of an undetected aneurysm while simply crossing the street. It wasn't fair....

But she still had her lovely ship, she had her work as Trade Minister, she had her friends, and she even had her own company, Kett Shipping. She would survive. But she would have been much happier if BeBob were there to help her connect the dots.

Soaring across the sky, the *Curiosity* left a bright and prominent vapor trail, which signaled her arrival to the uncommunicative people below. She skimmed past the high upper pastures and headed for the broad valley, the obvious population center of Happiness.

When the Klikiss swarms had returned a decade ago, surging through all of the open transportals, the sentient insects had overrun so many colonies, but somehow they had missed this place. Happiness looked pristine, though too quiet for her liking. Selecting a freshly harvested field, she landed the *Voracious Curiosity*, hoping this bare plot hadn't been freshly planted and that she had just ruined a season's worth of crops. Not the first impression she wanted to make.

When she emerged and walked down the ramp, she saw people moving toward her dressed in drab clothes and wide-brimmed hats. She planted her hands on her wide hips and drew a deep breath of "fresh" air filled with the scents of mown grass, mud, and manure. Her arrival caused quite a flurry.

Forty neo-Amish approached her, coming in from the fields or emerging from the homes. They didn't seem terrified, not unwelcoming. Despite the warm temperature, the women wore long skirts and full sleeves; the men had vests, long-sleeved shirts, long hair, and voluminous beards. They all carried hand implements for working the fields—rakes, hoes, shovels.

Although Rlinda found it quaint, she knew the charm would wear off after an hour or so. A few simple machines would have increased the crop yield and eliminated countless hours of backbreaking labor. Rlinda was not fond of backbreaking labor. But the people here did not seem downtrodden.

The tall fifty-ish man in the lead had long hair and a voluminous beard that spread out in wiry brown strands shot through with gray, which gave him an intense dramatic appearance, but his eyes were kind, his face was seamed, his hands were covered with a glove of calluses and dirt. "My name is Jeremiah Huystra, and I lead the people on Happiness. We wondered when you would come to find us."

Grinning, she stepped down off the ramp and extended her hand. "Somebody had to check up on you after the War. I'm Trade Minister Rlinda Kett. Sorry you fell through the cracks. I wanted to welcome you to the Confederation, make sure you weren't in need or in danger."

"We are not in danger," said Huystra. "and we do not need any interaction with the outside planets." His sonorous voice carried no threat, just a simple matter-of-fact tone.

"Glad to see your settlement is unscathed. A lot of terrible things have happened since you left the Hansa."

"We heard," said Huystra. "We've been visited several times in the past."

"Really? We have no record of that."

"It was not official. A Roamer clan leader named Olaf Reeves found us several years ago. His family offered us supplies and help, and by the requirements of hospitality we accepted their gifts. They accepted our explanation that we were doing fine, and they have left us alone."

A young man, twenty-five years old at the most, came forward. He had blond hair and handsome features that were hard to discern under the workaday grime and the curly beard that covered his cheeks. "Olaf Reeves told us about the Klikiss incursion, but the neo-Amish deactivated the transportal not long after establishing this settlement, so it seems we were lucky. Otherwise, the bugs would have taken over Happiness."

Rlinda narrowed her eyes and studied him. "You look familiar to me. I don't usually forget a face."

The young man looked embarrassed. "You don't know me anymore, but I was once Daniel. Prince Daniel. Chairman Wenceslas groomed me to take over from King Peter."

Rlinda drew back. She remembered that the young prince had mysteriously disappeared from Earth near the end of the War. "Prince Daniel! Well, it's good to see you again. The King and Queen will be thrilled to know you survived."

"They may be relieved to know I'm alive, but I'm not sure they would be thrilled." His voice took on a harder tone. "They're the ones who stranded me here. They stunned me and threw me through the Klikiss transportal."

Rlinda was scandalized. "I don't believe they told that part of the story."

The young man looked away, his cheeks flushing. "I deserved it. I was a real shit."

"Language," said Jeremiah Huystra in a quick stern tone.

"I would offer my apologies, Father Huystra, but that is the proper language. The King and Queen did what they had to do— and that brought me here. It turned out for the best."

As Daniel spoke, a young rosy-cheeked woman came forward to join him, taking his hand. She was pretty but plain, wearing dark blue skirts and a bonnet. She herded three young children, two boys and a girl.

"I would have been corrupted if I'd stayed back in the Hansa. I would have remained a bad person, an unfortunate person." He smiled at the young woman. "Now I have a lovely wife, Serene, and three beautiful children."

"Three, so far," said Serene, with a quirk of a smile.

"I wouldn't want to go back there." Daniel looked shyly at his wife, slipped his arm around her waist. "Getting exiled was truly the best thing that could ever have happened to me."

Huystra nodded somberly. "When he first arrived here, Daniel was quite a difficult young man, but exhaustion, contentment, and the inner satisfaction of a day's hard work cured him of that."

Chuckling, Rlinda looked around at the neo-Amish who stared at her and her ship. "This isn't the news I expected to hear, but I'm very glad for it."

"Stay for the evening meal," said Huystra. "We can tell you our stories. You will see exactly how our life is, but then we will ask you to keep our secret. We don't want to rejoin the Confederation. We have our Happiness."

CHAPTER TWO

Daniel

He had not thought about his past life in many years.

During his initial months trapped among the primitive neo-Amish, Daniel had been rebellious, angry, resistant and difficult. A real shit. Now in retrospect, when he thought about the person he'd been back at the Whisper Palace on Earth, being trained and twisted under the thumb of Chairman Wenceslas, brainwashed, deluded ... he would not have had it any other way. He did not want to leave here.

Father Huystra was justifiably concerned about the arrival of Captain Kett, but Daniel was more worried than any of them. Even back in the Hansa, the neo-Amish had never understood politics, business, or trade obligations. Completely insular, they had no grasp of how ambitious and determined people could be. The hydrogues, faeros, and even the Klikiss were destructive and dangerous, but not *devious*. They wouldn't try to wheedle their way into Happiness to trick or corrupt the neo-Amish.

Rlinda Kett seemed to have a good heart, though. Daniel remembered meeting her when he'd been groomed as Prince Daniel, because if he were to be the new king, he would need to interact with important traders. Vaguely recalling the woman's reputation, he realized that there could have been far more disastrous people to rediscover Happiness.

Even so, they had to be very careful to make sure she didn't spark a flood of well-intentioned Confederation representatives. The first ones would insist they were doing the right thing, and the second ones would overdo it, and by the third wave, the neo-Amish culture would be destroyed. That was why Jeremiah Huystra and his people had so eagerly gambled on the Klikiss colonization initiative and come here to this virgin planet. Hoping never to be found.

"This is delicious," Rlinda said, as she reached out to take the platter of roasted lamb chops. "Very earthy, simple yet flavorful." She speared some beets that dripped red onto her plate, then a serving of string beans. "Full of calories, but none of you looks fat," she said, bluntly. "Muscular, solid as a rock."

"We are the way life shapes us," Huystra said. "We work hard. We have a hearty life and devoted families."

"An admirable lifestyle," she said.

Daniel introduced her to Serene and their two sons, Malachi and Enoch, and their young daughter, Ruth, then he lowered his voice. "Please don't send anyone back here, Captain Kett. As you can see, life is perfect here. We're self-sufficient. Anything else would ruin it."

"I don't disagree, young man. The way I remember you is with fancy robes and fine jewels. You were pouty and demanded everything."

"I'm better now."

"Yes, you are," she agreed, and took another lamb chop. "I will make a notation in Confederation records that this colony is intact and in no need of assistance, then I'll bury the report. That's the best I can do." She spread her hands, and all the others nodded. She finished her meal, dabbed at her mouth with one of their rough napkins. "After this, I'm off to Rendezvous, going to see Olaf Reeves and his clan."

"Is he still rebuilding that old complex?" asked Huystra.

"Oh, I think he'll be rebuilding it for a very long time ... generations maybe. Any message you'd like me to bring to him?"

"Yes," Huystra said gruffly. "Thank him for not revealing our secret. Let us hope we can say the same about you, Rlinda Kett."

The trader woman promised, and rather than sleeping in a spare bedroom they offered, she chose to go back aboard her ship. "Time of day doesn't matter much when you're flying from star to star. I live by my own clock, and I prefer to sleep in my own bunk."

In the dark, Daniel and the neo-Amish followed her along the dirt streets to the empty field where she had landed, and they bid her farewell. The *Voracious Curiosity*'s engines brightened as the trading vessel lifted off, leaving deep marks in the field, then accelerated it reached higher altitude. The ship transformed into a bright shooting star that raced out into the universe.

Watching her go, Daniel let out a sigh of relief, glad the intruder was gone.

☾　•　☽

Next morning when he got up, ready for another day of hard work in the fields, Daniel dressed in clean clothes and ate the delicious breakfast Serene prepared—rich grainy bread, eggs, and potatoes to give him the energy he needed. Their morning conversation revolved around Captain Kett's visit and how the outsider woman had reminded him of his old life.

Serene had completely accepted him, as had all the neo-Amish. Yes, Daniel's life had been full of experiences back in the Whisper Palace with fine clothes and important diplomatic responsibilities as the supposed successor to the misbehaving King Peter. But once he had married beautiful Serene and settled into this comfortable and satisfying life insulated from the problems out in the Spiral Arm, he talked very little about what he had left behind.

He didn't withhold any information as a shameful secret, but his wife had been raised among the neo-Amish, and her curiosity extended no farther than what she could see with her own eyes. At first her simple complacency bothered him, but then Daniel realized that he didn't like to think of those things after all. Once he'd let himself become part of the community, once he contributed and benefited from the embrace of these people and their culture, he didn't miss his old life. Not at all. And he didn't miss who he had been.

Here on Happiness, he was rich in ways that he never knew to value before.

As the morning brightened. Daniel left the small cottage he shared with his family. The air was still fresh and brisk throughout the valley, and he would spend the day working in the communal cornfields weeding, hoeing, watching for unexpected blight.

His sturdy leather shoes made impressions in the soft dirt as he walked past their vegetable garden with tomatoes, squash, green peas, and okra. Serene kept her herb garden near the house so she could step outside and snip chives, or pull basil or rosemary for her cooking. Before school that morning, the children were supposed to be picking beans, but he found Malachi, Enoch, and Ruth fascinated with a strange new plant that had sprung up overnight.

Ruth glanced up at him and pointed toward the ground. "It looks funny, Dad, but pretty." She was smart and studious, the only one of the three children who didn't complain about lessons in the schoolhouse. Her two brothers poked at the growth.

Daniel bent to inspect the strange plant. It seemed halfway between a mushroom and a flower, a fleshy green stalk tipped with a hard, bullet-shaped purple capsule like an overripe eggplant. There were no leaves. He touched the cylinder—the bud? "It's not something we planted, so it must be native." He shooed the children away. "Go on, now, you have chores to do, beans to pick, then classes before noon."

Daniel trudged out into the fields of waist-high corn. He worked with a hoe to churn the soil between the rows, carefully extricating the weeds between the stalks. As the day warmed, the farmers mostly worked in congenial silence, though some hummed and others engaged in brief conversations.

Daniel let his thoughts wander. After Rlinda's visit he kept receiving flashes of young Peter and Estarra, his rivals—and what they had done to him, dumping him here on this backwater planet. But he understood their actions now. They had been desperate to keep themselves alive, aware that Chairman Wenceslas meant to eliminate them, replace them with a more pliable Daniel. He could not hold a grudge against them. The King and Queen could have killed him, but instead they exiled him. They had saved him.

Daniel looked up from his reverie, startled to find that the other farmers had stopped working, holding their hoes and tilting their wide-brimmed hats to look down the road. A lone man staggered down the path from the hills, which led to the smaller settlement in the upper meadows. Only a hundred people lived up in the alpine pastures compared to the four hundred down here in the main valley. This man staggered and swayed, stumbling along as if exhausted.

Jeremiah Huystra shaded his eyes and frowned. "This isn't right."

"It's Rickard," called one of the other farmers.

Then they were all rushing out to meet the man. His clothes were dirty, his hair disheveled; he had lost his hat somewhere along the road. His eyes were nearly swollen shut as if they'd been stung by wasps. Liquid oozed out of his ears, and his cheeks and chin were crusted with snot. Rickard coughed and sneezed, and he nearly collapsed, but the others held onto him. He was soaked with sweat.

"Are you sick, Rickard?" Jeremiah demanded. "Is it a fever? A plague?"

The man turned his face toward the sound, though he couldn't see. "No plague. Is that Father Jeremiah? Who is it?"

"It's Jeremiah." He grasped the shoulders of the weak and obviously sick man. "Tell us what happened."

Rickard said, "It's the spores. The grieka plants are rising again, just like ten years ago."

"Spores?" Daniel asked. "What spores?" He had heard the neo-Amish muttering about a great disaster in the colony's first year, but his brothers and sisters were reluctant to give any details.

Looking grave, Jeremiah turned to Daniel. "Grieka spores. Humans are extremely allergic to them. A great wave blossomed in our first year on Happiness, but then they died off, and they haven't bothered us since."

"Maybe they're cyclical," Daniel said.

They helped carry the weak man back toward the settlement. "In my home," Jeremiah said. "I have a spare bed."

Rickard continued to speak in his liquid, choking voice. "The sporeflowers began to rise two weeks ago, mostly around the ring of the meadows. The sheep ate them, and when the first few died we realized what the flowers were. Hundreds of them." When he shook his head, mucous dripped out of his nose. "Thousands! After the blossoms faded and the spore casings burst, spores filled the air, filled every breath. Toxic."

"Two weeks?" Daniel said. "If you saw them growing and you knew what they were, why didn't you come ask for help?"

"We prayed," said Rickard. Then he coughed and spat out a mouthful of phlegm just before they hauled him into Jeremiah's house. Several women emerged from their homes and hurried over to assist.

With a sidelong glance at Daniel, Jeremiah continued to explain. "We covered our mouths and noses, tried to stay inside until it passed, but the spores penetrated. Once the flowers burst and the toxins filled the wind, there was nothing we could do. We lost a third of our people in the spore storm."

"A third!" Daniel cried. "What if it's coming back?"

"Maybe the flowers will be limited to the high meadows this time," said Ezra, one of the other farmers.

"So many in the upper meadows are sick," Rickard said, then his knees gave out. They carried him into Jeremiah's home.

"Shouldn't we go help the other village?" Daniel asked.

Jeremiah shook his head. "The spores are already in the air. The healthy ones up there will have to take care of the sick, and we have to hope the griekas don't spread down here. We'll alert our people. They must pray as well and prepare themselves."

"There must be some other precautions we can take," Daniel said. He suddenly recalled the strange plant his children had found growing in their vegetable garden. He determined to chop it out of the ground, then burn it as soon as he got home.

"The spore storm will pass," Jeremiah said. "It did before." Three women brought moist rags and tended the sick man while Jeremiah and the farmers stepped outside, muttering together in deep concern. "It will pass. We will have to hunker down and endure."

Daniel thought of his beautiful wife, his three children. A third of the population had died from allergic reaction to the spores? *A third?* Statistically, that meant at least one member of his family would likely perish in the coming spore storm....

That night he was somber at dinner, and he held Serene tightly in bed. She clung to him. She had been here during the first spore storms, when she was just a girl. She didn't like to describe all the death, didn't like to think about it, so Daniel had to let his imagination paint dreaded pictures. Listening to a soft rain that pattered on the roof, he fell asleep in her arms.

When he woke, the air was fresh and sweet smelling, full of moisture. Stepping out of the house into the brightening dawn, he looked across the garden, the fields, the pastures and drew in a quick breath as he saw more of the strange purple buds rising up like mushrooms after a warm rain.

Thousands of them covering the ground, everywhere.

Everywhere.

CHAPTER THREE

Rlinda Kett

The Rendezvous asteroid cluster, formerly the government center for the Roamer clans, was a disorganized spray of rocks orbiting a red dwarf named Meyer. As the *Voracious Curiosity* approached, Rlinda thought the interconnected rocks still looked disorganized. That wasn't much of a surprise, since the Earth Defense Forces had blasted the complex apart and made the Roamers flee as outlaws during the Elemental War.

En route, Rlinda had prepared a particularly fine meal with fresh ingredients—potatoes, peas, beans, and carrots from Happiness. Though the neo-Amish liked to be isolated, their hospitality could not be faulted. Confident she would keep their secret, they were so trusting, so wholesome. Only Daniel, the former Prince, had shown any uneasiness. Rlinda remembered what a brat he had been, but she did admire how much he had changed.

She would respect the lost colony's wishes. Although she was a trader, as well as the Confederation's Trade Minister, she would leave them be and not let them be exploited by outside interests. Her goal was to keep everyone happy.

She now knew that Olaf Reeves had kept the secret as well, respecting the neo-Amish privacy. Roamer clans followed their Guiding Star, and the neo-Amish believed in a biblical God who somehow could not wrap His mind around post-industrial technology. But philosophically, the two groups were aligned, and it didn't surprise her that Olaf felt a certain kinship with them. The gruff old clan leader in the wreckage of Rendezvous wasn't very sociable either.

As the *Curiosity* cruised in, she picked up overlapping comm transmissions and the busy work of a bustling construction site. Before approaching the main asteroids, she made a point of identifying herself. Ever since Rendezvous had been attacked by the EDF, the Roamers had every reason to be jittery.

A young man responded on the comm screen. "This is Dale Reeves, Captain Kett. You are welcome here. We've restored an entire section of quarters on the tertiary asteroid, so there's plenty of room for you to visit."

"Give me a docking vector, and I'll be there in a jiffy." Relaxing back in her widened piloting seat, she tapped the silver capsule of BeBob's ashes. "It's good to be welcomed. Now let's see what these Roamers are up to."

She already knew Olaf's grand plans, since the gruff clan leader made no secret of his dreams, unorthodox though they might be. Rendezvous had once been an amazing island of habitable rocks, hollowed out and rigged with life-support systems. The clans had connected the asteroids with girders and walking tubes. At its peak, the grand complex had held nearly a hundred asteroids with outlying depots, tethered satellites, pressurized habitation warrens, and clan meeting centers. Rendezvous was where the various families discussed their business, and it was where their culture had blossomed.

Rlinda winced as space rubble pocked against her defensive shields. Much of Rendezvous had been blown up, hammered by EDF jazers. The broken pieces of an impressively complex puzzle had drifted aimlessly for years. Rlinda frowned at the idiocy of that chaotic massacre during the War, all the EDF Mantas and Juggernauts hunting down Roamer ships, when the actual enemies of humanity were the hydrogues and faeros....

She guided her ship toward a large crater in the central asteroid, which had been converted into a pressurized landing bay. Over millennia, the asteroid's surface had been marred by numerous celestial impacts, but she could make out dozens of fresh scars, patterns of disturbed regolith from recent explosions.

Since embracing the task of reconstructing Rendezvous, clan Reeves had maneuvered five of the main asteroids back together, building anchor struts, support girders, and reinforced tubes that let people travel from one rock to another without donning an exosuit. Right now she counted at least twenty construction workers outside attaching girders and stringing tethers so that smaller rocks could be pulled in to the central mass. Construction pods jetted around the expanse, pushing loose rocks inward.

Olaf's voice boomed over the comm. "Welcome, Captain Kett. It's about time someone from the Confederation came to see what we've accomplished."

"I'll be landing in five, and you can show me around."

She had already seen images of the progress. For the past decade, Olaf had been dogged in his determination to rebuild Rendezvous exactly as it had been, although the other Roamers had moved on, constructing a new government complex called Newstation. Not the most inspired of names, Rlinda thought, but descriptive at least.

Objectively, they had accomplished little in ten years, but the more the other clans rebuilt their holdings elsewhere, the more Olaf Reeves tightened his grip here, as if to prove he could accomplish what he had set out to do, whether or not it still made any sense.

After she landed the *Curiosity* inside the docking bay, an atmosphere containment field sealed over the gap, and she emerged as soon as the pressurization was complete. Roamers were already coming out to meet her.

A thin, nervous-looking young man accompanied the domineering Olaf Reeves. Olaf's voluminous beard was meticulously groomed, in sharp contrast to the unruly facial hair she had seen among the neo-Amish. Olaf smiled at her, but his face seemed tight, as if smiling was something he did only rarely. When she returned the gesture, she liked to think her smile was warmer and more sincere.

Other Roamers came out to join him as well as a tall, blond man with statuesque features and pale blue eyes. Olaf said to the blond man, "Bjorn, Captain Kett will need to have her ekti tanks refilled, and give her ship any maintenance it needs."

"The *Curiosity* will be fine," Rlinda said. "I brought you a nice gift." She held out the dirty cloth sack the farmers on Happiness had given her. Although she would have liked to keep all the fresh produce for herself, she knew how rarely the Roamers received real fruits and vegetables. "The neo-Amish on Happiness wanted me to give this to you."

Olaf reacted with surprise. "You've been to Happiness?" He looked around in alarm as if one of his people might have betrayed a confidence.

Rlinda held up a hand. "Nothing to worry about. I'll respect their privacy. As Confederation Trade Minister, I needed to make sure that the lost Klikiss colonies were at least accounted for. That's all I needed."

Olaf handed the sack of vegetables to his son, Dale, who passed them to a young woman hovering next to him. She was slender and pretty, with strawberry blond hair and eyes that flashed very quickly. She opened the sack and frowned inside at the turnips, sweet potatoes, cucumbers, and carrots, still covered with dried dirt.

Olaf gave her a dismissive gesture. "Sendra, go prepare a celebration meal for us. Do whatever you think best with the vegetables."

She sniffed. "I have no idea how to cook these. I don't even know what they are."

"Then you should learn if you intend to marry my son Garrison," Olaf scolded.

"Why would I need to learn that?" Blushing furiously, she held up a round turnip, turning it from side to side. "When would we ever grow one of ... these?"

Rlinda offered to cook them up. "I've got experience—and recipes."

Olaf seemed taken aback. "You and I have important matters to discuss, Captain Kett. If you are the Trade Minister, Rendezvous requires more materials, more funding, and more ships for the construction effort. If other clans had contributed to the work, we'd be much closer to completion by now."

Choosing her priorities, Rlinda reclaimed the sack of vegetables and then took Sendra's arm. "Important things first, Mr. Reeves. Anyone can do without politics, but we can't do without cooking." The young woman couldn't seem to decide whether to be miffed or relieved.

Later, surrounded by delicious aromas, Rlinda and Sendra presented the meal as if to a fine dignitary at her Arbor Restaurant on Theroc. Olaf had prepared a place for himself, another for Rlinda, and a third seat for Dale. Even though Sendra had helped cook, the clan leader did not invite her to join them. "This is business," he said, shooing her away. "When you're married to the future clan leader, you can join us. For now, let us talk."

Sendra frowned and flounced away.

After she left, Olaf's expression softened. "That's Sendra Detemer. She's had her eyes on my Garrison, and I think it'll be an acceptable match." A troubled look crossed his face. "Maybe she can bring my son back in line."

"Garrison's doing what he thinks best, Father," Dale said.

Olaf glared at his younger son. "He doesn't need to think what's best. I've already told him."

"Will Garrison be joining us for the discussion?" Rlinda asked, hoping it might soothe the obvious tension.

"No, he's off among the Roamer strongholds, gathering donations, materials, and trying to recruit workers." Olaf took several bites of his food without remarking on the taste at all, which disappointed Rlinda. "More than a decade a handful of us have been working here, just clan Reeves. Do the Roamers not remember their heritage? Don't they want us to be great again?"

Rlinda was surprised. "The Roamers are a respected part of human government now. They're no longer outlaws. Many clans are turning great profits."

"But it's not the same," Olaf said.

"Some might say the situation's improved," Dale said in a very small voice. He flinched as Olaf looked at him, but he added, "Roamers used to live only in the most hazardous environments. Now, we can live like normal people again."

"Roamers aren't normal people," Olaf said. "We're better. We develop survival skills that weaker members of the Confederation could never match. If we live under pampered conditions, we will forget what it is to be a Roamer." He nodded to himself. "A knife loses its edge unless it is sharpened."

Rlinda respected what clan Reeves had accomplished here, but rebuilding the entire complex seemed an insurmountable—and unnecessary—task.

"Newstation is quite remarkable," she pointed out. "A huge ring station above a planet that holds a Klikiss transportal. They've even parked a comet nearby so they can extract water and oxygen from the ices. It seems to be thriving." She hardened her voice, knowing what she had to do as Trade Minister. "In fact, many Roamer clans are wondering why you don't join the efforts there. Newstation is obviously going to be the main hub."

Olaf scoffed. "Rendezvous is where the first Roamers settled. This place is our history, and it's always been good enough for us."

"But it was just where a tired old colony ship encountered some rocks that could be made into a beachhead. Isn't that true?" Rlinda had studied a little bit of Roamer history, though most people in the Confederation were unaware of the details. "This place was an accident. Newstation was founded on purpose."

"Rendezvous is our home," Olaf said.

Hearing the finality in his tone, Rlinda gave him a conciliatory smile. "As Trade Minister, I'm just here to report. I don't take any sides in clan politics. Once Rendezvous is up and running again, you'll have plenty of people willing to come here to trade." She spread her hands. "Who says there needs to be only one big trading center? There can be Newstation, and there can be Rendezvous."

"And Ulio Station," Dale piped up. "There'll be a lot of trading complexes across the Spiral Arm. It shows how we're growing, recovering after the War. That's a good thing, isn't it?" He looked eagerly at his father.

Olaf simply frowned at his food. "Rendezvous is still our home."

Rlinda did her best to be polite for the rest of the meal, steering the conversation to news about strengthening ties with the Ildiran Empire, about how the Roamers were skymining again because hydrogues had not been seen on gas giants for nine years. She didn't mention the neo-Amish again, nor did she express that the more she saw of Olaf's work here at Rendezvous, the more she thought he was tilting at windmills.

Her greatest regret in coming here, though, was in sacrificing all those fresh homegrown vegetables. As far as she could tell, Olaf Reeves hadn't enjoyed a single bite.

CHAPTER FOUR

Garrison Reeves

On his regular supply run from Rendezvous, Garrison Reeves set a new course in the battered old clan ship, the *Workhorse*. He headed off to a system that was not only unexpected, but completely forbidden, according to his father. Garrison did it anyway.

He had been flying the clan ship on solo missions since he was seventeen, because there was so much work to be done at the construction site. The asteroids were scattered, but Garrison's father would not turn his attention from his plan—his obsession—to rebuild the place. Garrison had spent years believing in the dream himself, swept up in his father's enthusiasm and determination. But the task was insurmountable ... and unnecessary.

Once, a year ago, Olaf had taken Garrison out in an inspection pod, flying around the drifting asteroids. In the cockpit he displayed a projection of how the main components could all be reconnected one rock at a time. "They'll be refurbished with life-support systems and power blocks, and we'll open up a warren of living quarters, just like it once was." The big bearded man had gestured out into the glittering points of light in the starscape.

"As the next clan head, this task will fall to you, Garrison. I doubt it'll be completed in my lifetime, especially since the other clans have abandoned our work. But the responsibility falls on you. Follow your Guiding Star. The end result will be worth it."

When he was younger, Garrison had been just as angry that the clans had lost interest and moved on, choosing to build an advanced new trading hub rather than staying with their old home. Before long, though, he decided that his father's glorious vision had simply become a stubborn delusion. And the more Garrison flew missions to Roamer outposts, speaking with traders and Confederation representatives, he began to make up his own mind.

Because Olaf Reeves had such an abrasive personality and tended to dominate conversations, Garrison was often a better mouthpiece to get their point across. He would go to Newstation and talk about the coming golden age of Rendezvous, but amidst the obvious success and energy of Newstation and the Roamer offices run by Speaker Del Kellum, Garrison saw more amusement than excitement in their responses.

He had recently spoken to one plump and wealthy trader who had brought in a load of exotic alien fabrics from the Ildiran Empire. "Young man, if Olaf would just bring your clan's dedication and hard work *here*, we'd finish Newstation in no time."

"But Rendezvous is our history," Garrison had quoted, as expected. "Our heritage."

"I can read about history and heritage in a book. I've got a business to run."

Unfortunately, Garrison's heart wasn't in it, and he no longer believed the arguments himself, so he didn't bother making a rebuttal.

This time, after leaving Newstation, he made an extreme and intentional detour. Olaf would know about it if he ever reviewed the navigation logs, but Garrison didn't care. He had to stand up for himself if he was going to be the next leader of clan Reeves.

This time, he flew the *Workhorse* directly to Earth.

(•)

Though the world was a place of legend, Garrison had never been to the birthplace of humanity, the origin point from which thirteen huge generation ships had been launched centuries ago. Earth was a place of legend. Now, he hoped it would be a place to solve his family's problems. He intended to find exactly what clan Reeves needed to finish the Rendezvous construction project.

Approaching Earth, he was careful to negotiate the navigational hazards posed by the destroyed Moon, the vast rubble field strewn in a broad swath along its former orbit. Nine years ago the faeros had blasted the Moon into shards of wandering rock that still drifted about; many had struck Earth in deadly meteor impacts.

Now, though, the rubble was abuzz with dozens of large Confederation Defense Forces battleships, Manta cruisers, and even two Juggernauts, as well as hundreds of commercial ships, trading vessels, industrial units, and construction centers. The CDF was building a large military complex among the lunar fragments, making use of the unlimited metals and ores to be extracted from the rocks. Many Roamers had volunteered for the work, which fit perfectly with their skills.

The sheer blur of activity, exuberance, and manpower reminded Garrison just how small the Rendezvous reconstruction project was. If he could make the proper connections here, he could find exactly the help they needed.

But, oh, his father would hate it!

He flew the *Workhorse* among the space traffic patterns, wary of the tumbling, sharp-edged rocks. So much destruction ... and Olaf Reeves insisted that the people of Earth had caused it themselves.

Garrison remembered the last and most vehement argument with his father over the very principle. He knew the Confederation was willing to help, and the Roamers—including clan Reeves—were part of the Confederation.

"The Hansa is gone now, Father," he had said. "We should join the community for the benefit of all, not hide here and grumble about lost days."

Olaf had fumed. "The Hansa is the root of all our problems! Chairman Wenceslas declared war on us for his own purposes. He sent EDF battleships to destroy Rendezvous purely out of spite, because we wouldn't bow to his commands. It was because of *his* corrupt leadership and his provocations that the faeros destroyed the Moon! They caused the disaster, and they have to live with the consequences of their actions." His face grew red. "But *we* don't have to participate. I would never accept help from them."

"The Hansa no longer exists," Garrison repeated. "We're the Confederation now. We should look forward."

"If you look forward, you might not see the knife coming toward your back," Olaf said with a huff. "We will have no dealings with Earth. We will not help them, nor will we ask for their help. They brought this destruction upon themselves."

Incensed, Garrison had said, "But Rendezvous was destroyed too. Look around you, our asteroid cluster blasted apart, all those people dead, all those clans scattered. How is that different from the Moon being destroyed? Did we bring *this* on ourselves? Are *we* to blame?"

Olaf reached out and slapped him across the face. Hard. "I will not have insubordination from my own son. When you become clan leader, you can tell your own sons what to do, and if I raised you right, you will see your Guiding Star clearly. For now, you will do as I command."

Garrison had pretended to be dutifully obedient after that, at least on the outside. He did his trading runs, he mumbled his inspirational speeches, he attempted to get funding to expand the Rendezvous effort, although when he did receive money, it was usually a donation instead of a loan, because the wealthy Roamers knew that clan Reeves wouldn't be able to pay them back.

The more Olaf insisted that Earth was forbidden, however, the more Garrison researched it, the more he observed what those people were doing in the rubble of their Moon and how those efforts could be copied at Rendezvous. By using efficient new modules to piece together an operations center and habitation complexes, they had accomplished more in the first two years than clan Reeves had done in nearly a decade....

Now, the *Workhorse* fit right in among the other Roamer vessels. The Earth ships were shiny, recent models, many constructed after the end of the War. Impeller tugs moved the orbiting rubble while mobile smelters created new materials that were used to build free-floating space stations or domes. Tunnel warrens were burrowed inside the larger rocks. He saw hundreds of identical-looking prefabricated modules forming the new habitation complexes.

Using such ubiquitous, and presumably inexpensive, modules, Garrison imagined his clan could rebuild Rendezvous and open it up to business and habitation in a few months. Those mass-produced modules would shave years or even decades from Olaf's construction plan. The finished complex would not look exactly the same as the former Rendezvous, but it would be functional— and Roamers were supposed to adapt.

He nosed around the lunar orbital complex, spoke with contract Roamer construction crews, even tracked down one of the main engineers to ask about the modules. The engineer said, "They're manufactured by an Earth-based industrialist who was a Roamer clan member. I bet you can work out a deal."

"A former Roamer?" Garrison had never heard of such a thing.

"Oh, Lee Iswander is still a Roamer, though he now wears business suits. Iswander Industries manufactures these modules. I bet he'd extend credit for another Roamer family, especially in the name of Rendezvous. We all still have a soft spot in our heart for that place." The engineer chuckled. "Though I've heard tell that Olaf Reeves has a soft spot in his head."

☾　•　☽

Flying in, he was overwhelmed by the enormity of the cities, the towering skyscrapers, the flying craft in the skies, the people crowded in the streets, the water, the trees, the clouds. Roamers had always lived in crowded conditions with tight resources. Even their thriving colonies were sparsely populated, young but growing.

Earth was ... tremendous, and he drank it all in.

He tracked down the headquarters tower of Iswander Industries—which he learned later was merely one of many, since the industrialist had set up diversified businesses in numerous other systems, using Roamer talents to innovate old processes.

29

After identifying himself, Garrison was surprised to be granted a brief meeting—ten minutes only—with Lee Iswander himself.

When he arrived, on time, he found Iswander sitting at his desk, with a woman sitting beside him in a guest chair. She was maybe five years older than Garrison, trim and beautiful with auburn hair and gold-flecked green eyes. Her beauty was unmarred by any smile or softness, but he immediately noticed that she had a depth to her.

As Garrison entered the office, Iswander stood and extended his hand across the desk, though his expression was skeptical. He was tall and fit, with dark brown hair frosted with gray at the temples. "The last person I expected to see in Iswander Headquarters is the son of stick-in-the-mud Olaf Reeves."

Garrison wondered if the industrialist was trying to insult him or tease him, although his tone seemed neutral. He answered spontaneously. "I am not my father, Mr. Iswander."

Softening his expression, the industrialist sat back at his desk. "Glad to hear it, Mr. Reeves. Roamers need to look forward now, and many of my workers are clan members. The old ways have been wrecked, thanks to the hydrogues, the faeros, and the Klikiss. But we can rebuild—if we have the will to do so. We have the whole future ahead of us, and fossils have no place in our forward motion." He introduced the silent woman at his side. "This is my deputy, Elisa Enturi."

Elisa formally extended her hand, and Garrison took it. She seemed to look past and through him. "Your jumpsuit is ... interesting."

He brushed at his chest, looked at the embroidered clan markings, his pockets, zippers, and clips. He sensed that her comment was not a compliment.

Iswander laughed. "Don't criticize his attire, Elisa. There's very little cause for a suit and a tie in a space construction site, and rebuilding is what we do." He narrowed his eyes. "Is that what you're doing, Mr. Reeves?"

"My father is. We're trying to rebuild Rendezvous."

Elisa rolled her eyes, and Iswander let out a low groan in his throat. "To what purpose? Nostalgia isn't a good enough business reason to make such an investment in time, money, and effort."

Garrison shrugged. "I don't disagree. That's why I've come to you for help. I think Iswander Industries may have a solution. I've seen your prefabricated modules—I assume you're manufacturing them in large quantities?"

"Massive quantities," Iswander said, "and they're designed to be easily transportable. We have them emplaced on more than forty planets, colonies damaged in the War, where the people are seeking to rebuild."

Garrison said, "At Rendezvous we have refurbished and reconnected four of the orbiting rocks, but there are dozens more to go. It'll take years. With your modules, though, we could be open and functioning in no time." He swallowed. "I have a line of credit from clan Reeves."

Elisa broke in. "Newstation is almost finished. Won't that be the Roamer government headquarters? It's where Speaker Kellum set up his offices."

"Newstation appears to be thriving," Garrison admitted, "but there's no reason Rendezvous can't be a headquarters as well."

"Or a museum," Iswander said.

"Or a museum," Garrison said, "a heritage site. My father won't be convinced otherwise, and so I'm here to look for help. If you and I can work out a deal, it would benefit all the Roamer clans."

"It would certainly benefit clan Reeves," Iswander said. "Your father has not said very kind things about me. Because I am a businessman and because I look for industrial opportunities, he compares me to Chairman Wenceslas." He tugged on his collar, his tie. "Because I wear this instead of a dirty old jumpsuit."

"My father says you're not a Roamer inside anymore. I don't necessarily agree, but if you do arrange for the modules to go to Rendezvous, that would convince the other clans that your heart is still with us."

Iswander snorted and rearranged papers on his desk. "I don't make business decisions with my heartstrings, Mr. Reeves. If you want me to provide modules, then let's see what kind of credit and financing you have, what sort of down payment you bring."

Garrison smiled. "Good, let's have a business discussion, then. At Newstation I recently received substantial donations from four clans and even a note of appreciation from Speaker Kellum." He handed Iswander the note.

Elisa just watched Garrison, barely blinking. She didn't seem impressed.

Iswander skimmed it. "That's well and good, but I am not Speaker, nor do I ever intend to be. I am a businessman, and the Roamers are part of the Confederation now. I have to look at the bigger picture."

Garrison leaned forward, eager. "I agree, let's look at a big picture. My father taught me to have ambitious plans. I'd just like to be more realistic about accomplishing them."

Iswander glanced at the time displayed on his wall and gave a quick nod of dismissal. "You and Elisa can go over the numbers and find a realistic answer, then. I'll make the deal happen if it makes sense."

CHAPTER FIVE

Elisa Enturi

After Garrison Reeves had presented his case and departed, Lee Iswander had other pressing business concerns. Elisa remained at his side helping to navigate them. When she had begun working for him several years ago, Elisa determined to make herself indispensable, and she had done that quickly enough, but once she achieved that goal, she saw so much more to be done.

"We must always keep our eyes open for opportunities," Iswander said. He used the phrase so often it was practically his mantra.

Now, he looked at her and mused, "I've never been impressed with Olaf Reeves and his backward-thinking clan, but young Garrison seems a different sort. He has his sights set firmly on the future. We should encourage that."

Elisa nodded. "And the friction between himself and his father is obvious."

Iswander gave her a thin smile as he stood from his desk. "If our participation helps nudge Olaf Reeves back into the mainstream, then all the better. Arrange the deal Garrison needs, will you, Elisa?"

"Of course, sir." She was already considering how to divert a cluster of surplus, old-model modules that had remained unsold, and she also knew how she could use more of those modules as leverage for a project of her own....

We must always keep our eyes open for opportunities.

She leaned over the desk, called up a new file. "I wanted to show you a report of an extreme new planetary system. Iswander Industries may wish to exploit. Facilities, construction, and maintenance will be a challenge, but I believe it has great potential for metals extraction."

Amused, Iswander raised his eyebrows. "I come from Roamer stock, Elisa. 'Challenging' is what we do best. What did you have in mind?"

"Sheol is a binary planet, uninhabited—and uninhabitable, far enough from its sun that it falls within the Goldilocks temperature range, but the two halves orbit so closely together that tidal stresses create great seismic upheaval. The surface is molten, and metals from deep underground churn to the surface."

She watched his eyes light up as he saw what she was getting at. "In other words, we don't have to build a smelting facility or refinery? We don't have to mine? All we have to do is scoop up the valuable metals floating there?"

"That's right, sir—if we can find a way to build reinforced operations." She displayed orbital and planetary diagrams for the Sheol system, as well as images from unmanned probes. "According to the initial samples, it's more than plain metals, but also exotic alloys, crystal and metal blends created under extreme conditions, mixed with a liberal dash of fresh radioactive isotopes from below."

Iswander skimmed the columns of numbers, graphs of materials found, projections of profits. "Sounds like an industrial paradise, even if the place is named after hell."

She controlled her satisfied smile. "Do I have your permission to investigate it as a possible industrial property, sir?"

He reacted as if she'd asked him a foolish question. "You know you've made a convincing case. We must always keep our eyes open for opportunities."

She smiled when he said that.

He went to the rear door of his office. "Come with me. Let's take a shuttle up to orbit and head out to the lunar operations. I want to see our construction operations there."

"Everything's progressing on schedule, sir," Elisa said, following him to the rooftop landing platform.

"Of course it is, but the boss who isn't fundamentally aware of his major projects is not a good boss."

He had told her that before too, and Elisa took it to heart.

Iswander Industries had contracted to assemble a new base for the Confederation Defense Forces, but he also had plans for commercial and civilian operations in lunar orbit, intending to open a hotel and recreational complex.

As they rode together in their high-acceleration vehicle, which looped around the planet and transferred to lunar orbit, Elisa searched for a way to propose her own plan. She had no reason to believe Iswander would turn her down, but this was the first genuinely personal idea she had presented, a plan that would increase her importance in Iswander Industries.

Sitting in the seat, he occupied himself with a datapad, scrolling through summary reports for dozens of allied industrial operations. She leaned closer to him as the ship flew smoothly onward. "Sir, you previously talked about the great benefit of tourism and luxury hotels, even in the lunar rubble belt."

He nodded, not yet paying full attention to her. "Yes, tourism is one of the most profitable industries in human civilization."

"Then I'd like to try something, sir—a new kind of resort, a new kind of sightseeing in a new place."

He let out a good-natured laugh. "From what I've seen, there's no place in the Spiral Arm that hasn't been tapped by some ambitious, if possibly ill-advised, entrepreneur."

She called up images on her own datapad. "Not this place, sir—not since the hydrogues." That caught his attention. She called up the colorful image of a gas giant striped with swirling cloud bands. "After the hydrogues attacked so many Roamer skymines and drove humans from the gas planets, few people have gone back there. They're empty, unclaimed. Ready for us."

Iswander pursed his lips, studying the images she showed him. "I've heard that a handful of Roamer clans have set up skymining operations again. No incidents, as far as I know."

"Exactly, sir. I'm considering a prototype 'sky hotel,' a drifting resort amid the colorful clouds of some temperate gas giant."

"Who would want to go to such a place?"

Elisa pulled up more images, talking faster now. "It could be marketed as a serene luxury resort, drifting high above the cloud bands. Maybe even find a chemical mixture in the rising gases with alleged 'health benefits'—like mineral spas or hot springs—and charge extra."

Iswander considered the idea, deep in thought, but she continued, "With your permission, I would use four surplus modules, connect them into a free-floating city above the clouds of a placid gas giant, bring in a small staff. Then we'd offer test lodgings for a handful of people, as a proof of concept."

"Sounds hazardous," Iswander pointed out. "Just because we haven't seen the hydrogues in years, we know they still live deep in the gas planets. What if they come up and destroy everything? What about the risks?"

"I intend to make that my selling point," Elisa said, surprising him. "You're not looking at the hazard with the right spin. I'd appeal to thrill-seekers and characterize the dangers as *assets*."

"That's ridiculous," he said, but there was no sting in his tone. "But I've observed quite often that people are ridiculous."

"I have already developed a business plan and sent out some feelers, sir. I've found four people willing to try the test run—for a reduced rate, of course."

Now Iswander was interested.

Their shuttle approached the glittering lights scattered among the lunar rubble. Illuminated by sunlight reflecting off fresh metals and regolith scars, the swath of new asteroids looked like a miniature version of the Milky Way.

Iswander mused, "I spend little time with the Roamer clans these days. I try to bring them opportunities, but I also want to make a profit and build my businesses in unorthodox ways. Your sky hotel sounds like a very Roamer thing to do, Elisa." She maintained a flat expression, not sure that he meant it as a compliment, then he added, "I'm proud of you."

"Thank you, sir."

"When we ship sixteen of our surplus modules to Rendezvous so clan Reeves can use them in their reconstruction efforts, let's make it an even twenty, with the other four allocated to you. Do we have the assets in place?"

Elisa was surprised. "Yes, sir."

"Good. We'll slip those four into the paperwork. Find a couple of volunteers among my employees, then go prove your concept. Build a hotel in the clouds and show me we can turn a profit. Come to me when it's finished."

She felt a flush of excitement. "I won't let you down, Mr. Iswander. This could be quite lucrative."

He looked at her with his wise expression. "All business ventures *could* be lucrative, Ms. Enturi. Unfortunately, most of them fail. Let this be your way of proving yourself. Demonstrate your vision and your administrative capabilities. But whatever happens, don't make Iswander Industries look bad. If you manage that, I'll be satisfied enough."

(•)

After returning home, Elisa felt like celebrating, even as her mind filled with plans for her sky-hotel concept. She accessed the personnel records of local Iswander employees, as well as a winnowed list of possible gas giants.

She sat alone in a noisy, colorful bar near Iswander Headquarters, sipping a goblet of rich clove-flavored wine imported from New Portugal. It was expensive stuff, and Elisa didn't normally pamper herself. But tonight she had reason to acknowledge what she had achieved.

She quickly selected the swollen planet Qhardin, a gas world with a temperate climate and an atmospheric composition that, at the right altitude, was breathable, though cold. Qhardin was a world currently unexploited by Roamer industries, although several cloud harvesters remained adrift, damaged and abandoned after the hydrogue depredations during the War. She decided those wrecks would make interesting "ghost town" tours for her thrillseeker clientele.

The prefabricated modules would be easily assembled, per design, and would require very little maintenance. Elisa didn't want to manage a large crew. A competent engineer, as well as cooking and serving staff—two, she decided—would be all she needed for her first test run. She scrolled through employee records and narrowed down her choices. In the past half hour, she had already diverted the four surplus modules and arranged for them to be shipped to Qhardin. They would be launched as soon as she finalized her employee choices.

"May I join you?" asked a friendly male voice. "We both have something to celebrate."

Garrison Reeves no longer wore his Roamer jumpsuit, but instead had changed into normal Earth clothes, probably bought for the occasion. She saw his warm and inviting expression.

When she worked away from her offices and distractions, she was often able to fade into the background and think. Elisa genuinely wanted to be alone, to concentrate, but she thought better of chasing him away. She nodded toward the empty chair at her small table. "If we're going to be business partners, we should get to know each other better."

He indicated her half-empty goblet of wine. "Can I buy you another drink?"

"Are you asking whether I will allow you to? Or whether you can actually afford it?"

"It depends on what you're drinking," he said.

"Expensive stuff."

He faltered a little, but then his back straightened. "Yes, I can afford it. Does that mean you will allow it?"

She smiled. "Of course, Mr. Reeves."

"And I'll have one with you."

"Do you have a taste for good wine? I didn't know Roamers drank the stuff."

"If that's what you're drinking, I'm sure I'll enjoy it."

"I hope so, otherwise it would be quite the waste."

They ordered two more glasses and sat talking. His stories about eking out a living in the empty old clan government complex alarmed her. Garrison didn't even seem to realize how unnecessarily austere and difficult those years had been. Lee

Iswander had told her about the Roamers, but he was a different sort of Roamer.

"You should come see for yourself," Garrison said. "In its heyday, Rendezvous really was quite a magnificent place."

"It'll never have the same heyday again. Now that you've seen Earth with your own eyes, can you still brag about Rendezvous?"

His expression fell. "Not really. Are you a Roamer, too? Is that why Iswander hired you?"

She stiffened. "Not at all. I was born and raised here on Earth to a poor family, but I worked my way up." She heaved a sigh. "My parents and my brothers didn't want to make anything of themselves. I worked hard, earned a little more, and my family spent it, as if it was their due. They wanted handouts, not opportunities. When they did have a chance to make extra money or improve their lives, they found excuses, then they complained about other people getting ahead." She made a disgusted noise.

She finished her wine, while Garrison nursed his, either because he didn't like it, or because he wasn't eager to pay for another round. She stood. "Let's go out on the observation balcony. According to orbital tracking, we're due for a good burst of meteors tonight."

"I've never seen a meteor shower." To her surprised look, he added, "Remember, I grew up where there was no atmosphere. Is it dangerous? I know about all the cities that were wiped out."

"Not tonight. Mapping shows nothing larger than half a meter in diameter and nothing that should survive all the way to the surface."

On the outer deck on the bar's tenth floor, they gathered with other patrons, all of them cradling drinks, chatting calmly as they watched the starry skies suffused with the fog of city lights. It was a slow buildup, but soon bright scratches streaked overhead as fragments of the broken Moon burned up in the atmosphere. The crowd gasped at a particularly bright bolide that sizzled and popped across the sky, followed by a fast-moving screamer that whistled itself into silence as it was incinerated.

Garrison cheered more than anyone else, delighted like a child.

Elisa felt her nerves on edge. Yes, this was a beautiful display, but she could not forget those initial terrible nights after the destruction of the Moon. Huge chunks drawn in by Earth's gravity had plummeted through the sky to smash cities like Madrid and Buenos Aires, making the human race huddle in terror.

Those who had the means to do so evacuated Earth, but Elisa's family was poor. They had squandered their spare money on useless things, and now they had no way to protect themselves. Elisa was trapped with them, dreading that the next roaring sound they heard would be their last. She never wanted to feel so helpless again.

She left her family after that, abandoning them to their own failures and lack of ambition. She had clawed her way up in Iswander Industries, making herself important. She was no longer poor, but the money didn't matter to her. She was no longer *powerless*, and that was what she clung to.

She and Garrison watched the meteor shower for more than an hour. Elisa slipped inside to buy them both another drink, cautiously beginning to believe that she might have something in common with this Roamer dreamer after all.

CHAPTER SIX

Rlinda Kett

Back at the Earth headquarters of Kett Shipping, Rlinda was glad to settle into her offices again. She was still the magnate of her trading empire, but she couldn't devote much time to administering the company because she had her duties as Trade Minister. But King Peter and Queen Estarra had made allowances for her. Rlinda was not a politician, nor did she want to be. Hell, she didn't even want to be the manager of her own company, but certain things couldn't be avoided.

After changing her clothes, Rlinda replaced the silver capsule of BeBob's ashes on its stand on her desk, then she ate a private four-course meal in her penthouse offices. She got ready to meet with her visitors—Tasia Tamblyn and Robb Brindle, who were both extremely competent pilots and who had distinguished themselves during the War.

"Rlinda, you're back home," said Robb. "We missed you."

"You missed my cooking, you mean," Rlinda said.

"Actually," Tasia said, "we missed the *Voracious Curiosity*. We've grown so fond of that ship, the other alternatives just aren't the same. Can we have it back now? We've got some runs to make."

"The *Curiosity* is still mine, kids. Just because I let you borrow it, doesn't mean it belongs to you." Rlinda got up and walked around her desk to greet the eight-year-old boy who accompanied Tasia and Robb. "And there's little Xander. Does he have his pilot's license yet?"

"Not yet," the boy said. "I'm still studying. Maybe by the time I'm ten."

Xander had been born aboard the *Curiosity* during one of Tasia and Robb's runs. The boy spent more time aboard the ship than on the surface of any planet. Tasia was the daughter of a well-known Roamer clan, and Robb was a former officer in the Earth Defense Forces.

"You're welcome to come along with us to Newstation," Robb said. "We're going to see Tasia's brother, Jess."

Rlinda bent over, still paying more attention to the boy. "Have you ever met your uncle, Xander?"

"Of course. He's famous."

"A lot of us were famous, my dear boy, but that isn't always as fun as it might sound."

"We've all been to Newstation," Tasia said, "and now we need to go back for some business."

"Tasia wants to be Speaker of the clans someday," Robb teased.

His wife shot him a quick glare. "Shizz, not on your life! Del Kellum can have the position."

"He won't be Speaker forever," Rlinda said.

"And I won't be Speaker at all," Tasia replied. "But we do want to see Jess. He and Cesca are forming a school inside the hollow comet near the station. It should be a sight to see. And you should go along, Rlinda, because as Trade Minister, you need to meet with the Speaker of the clans, since most Confederation trade comes from the Roamers."

Rlinda knew it was true. "You make a compelling argument ... even though I did just get home." She sighed. "I wanted to relax, cook a few meals, tour my restaurant."

"We'll take the *Curiosity* without you, then," Robb said, "and we'll report back."

"You will not take the *Curiosity*. I'm going with you. Just give me a day to take care of loose ends."

Rlinda was already considering her favorite meals to cook, then decided that was better left to her professional chefs. "We're all going to dinner, my treat. We'll order a selection of items off the menu—for quality-control purposes." She tousled the boy's hair, much to Xander's annoyance. "We want this young man to grow up with a distinguished palate."

"Shizz, distinguished or not, I'm happy for a free meal," Tasia joked.

"And the conversation," Robb added.

"We'll stuff ourselves," Rlinda said. "Then we can digest it all on the flight to Newstation."

CHAPTER SEVEN

Daniel

Budding grieka plants covered the valley and the hills, spreading, growing. If Daniel hadn't known what they were, he might have found them lush and beautiful. They would blossom soon and spread death.

The spores must have lain dormant inside the soil until something triggered this explosive growth. It might well have been a natural cycle on Happiness, a surge that occurred every decade or so, but since the colonists had only been there for a dozen years total, they were unfamiliar with the regular recurrence.

Daniel vowed he would not lose a third of the people he knew here!

Rickard, the sick man from the alpine meadows, died the day before, which brought sorrow but no surprise, considering his condition. Everyone had seen his swollen eyes as well as the pus and mucous leaking from his face. Father Jeremiah insisted on a formal funeral, quickly done, with spoken prayers and sung hymns. They all knew that before long there would be too many funerals to count.

Daniel's heart ached with dread as he watched the grim, frightened farmers staring at the alien growths that infested their arable land. With a sick feeling, he stood outside his family home in the cool morning, breathing the fresh air but knowing that the air might already be laden with the potentially toxic spores.

A faint mist hung in the low-lying areas of the valley. Some neo-Amish farmers were out tending their fields, while their wives took care of the vegetable gardens or the livestock. The whole village seemed either oblivious or determined to ignore the peril.

Daniel had tried to urge them into action, but no one could decide what action to take. Many of the Happiness colonists prayed, though they admitted that would likely not be enough. It certainly hadn't been sufficient the last time. Others simply went through their days with a fatalism, knowing what was to come from the spore storms, but convinced they would somehow survive ... or at least a certain percentage of them would.

With her quiet and shy demeanor, Serene came out onto the porch. She held a metal cup of strong coffee she had boiled. "For your morning, my husband."

He accepted the hot cup, which burned the tips of his callused fingers. He leaned close to touch her shoulder with his, glad for the closeness of her. His wife. The mother of his children. The first person to make his exile tolerable and then wonderful. He would not lose a third of the people he knew here!

The children were out playing, although Daniel felt a deep dread, not wanting them to touch the grieka plants—but they were everywhere. Daniel nodded toward the far side of the valley, where black smears of smoke wafted into the sky. "Look, Serene. The Van Deens are burning all their fields."

"They argued with Jeremiah. We usually listen to him, because he is often right." She looked at Daniel with a bleak expression. "But not this time."

"Neither side of that argument was correct," Daniel said.

The Van Deens and four other families wanted the neo-Amish to engage in an extreme eradication effort, chopping down and burning any grieka plants they found. Daniel applauded the fact that they were taking action, while Jeremiah insisted that his people could not thwart the will of God.

Under other circumstances Daniel would have been with the Van Deens, torching the ground to kill the grieka plants, but from his own quick scouting expeditions into the hills, he saw the prominent fleshy sporeflowers everywhere, a carpet from this valley to the next, probably across the whole continent. They were unstoppable. Once the grieka flowered and burst, the skies would be filled with spores, and the winds would carry the dust everywhere. Burning a few acres would do nothing to diminish the threat.

Still, how could they not do *something*? How could the people just stand here and accept their fates? Daniel knew the neo-Amish all too well, and accepting their fate was exactly how they viewed life. They were passengers through their existence, guided by God.

After being torn from his ostentatious and spoiled life as a Hansa prince, Daniel had gradually accepted his situation. He'd grown to admire the neo-Amish for how they purged stress and conflict from their lives with a purity of acceptance. Daniel gritted his teeth. He would not accept that fatalism now.

His children did not understand the tension throughout the colony. All three ran about with the carefree exuberance of children, and their delighted outcries attracted Daniel's attention. They had found something near the garden.

He and Serene left the porch went to see what had drawn their attention. Ruth was bending down on her skinned knees to look at a particularly tall grieka plant. The fleshy bud had cracked open to display spotted pink petals. "It's a pretty flower!"

In alarm, Daniel grabbed his daughter's skinny arm and yanked her roughly away. "Don't touch that!" Startled, Ruth was ready to burst into tears. The two boys were wide-eyed at their father's tone. "Stay away from those flowers—all of them!"

Leaving the children with Serene, he ran to retrieve his hoe and hacked the plant apart, as if he could accomplish something by directing his anger at this one target. He felt sick inside.

He saw Father Jeremiah leave his house, dressed in work clothes and wide-brimmed hat. He headed toward the fields to do his daily work, as if this were any other morning. Daniel strode up to him. "Father Jeremiah, do you have records of the last outbreak? What did you learn? You must have studied the grieka plants—what is their life cycle? How fast do they blossom?"

How much time do we have? was what he really wanted to ask.

The neo-Amish had practical midwives, healers, and herbalists, but they conducted no medical research nor any scientific studies beyond what was necessary for agriculture in their daily lives.

Jeremiah looked at him as if he had spoken in an incomprehensible language. "They are plants. They grow, they mature, and spread their spores. They are part of this planet, and we are just visitors. Sometimes it is difficult."

"And sometimes a problem can be solved," Daniel insisted.

When Jeremiah just gave him a blank look, Daniel pleaded, "Are there journals at least? Descriptions of the symptoms, how people are exposed to the spores? Which ones get sick and which ones don't? Was there any pattern?"

Jeremiah's heavy eyebrows drew together, and he shook his head. "The ones who survived are all around you—that much is obvious. The ones who died are buried in the cemetery on the hill."

Daniel hardened his voice. "I know, I've been up there. I counted the graves, and I looked at the names. We're going to need a lot more graves after this outbreak."

The leader nodded solemnly. "Yes, Daniel, we will."

"But what if there's a way we could prevent it? How did you try to treat the people last time? Did anything work? We need to prepare *now*."

"We did what we could." Jeremiah scratched his beard. "We wore scarves over our mouths and noses. We stayed inside our homes. We washed ourselves and tried to stay free from the spores. But once all the flowers blossomed, the spores were like a fog in the valley. There is no way to fight it." He leaned closer, dropped his voice. "Daniel, you and your family should prepare. It is certain that some of us will not survive the spore storms. You should pray, tell your wife and children how much you love them, and then hope."

"Hope is not enough," Daniel said.

"Hope is always enough." Jeremiah seemed to be quoting a platitude, rather than stating anything of use.

Daniel refused to accept it. "I've never regretted leaving the Hansa. Once I turned my back on civilization, I realized how irrelevant all those luxuries were. But what if the solution is something simple? What if all we need to survive are respiratory filters and door seals? What if a common antihistamine could cure us? We owe it to our people to investigate that possibility."

"And how would you investigate it?" Jeremiah said. "We have no research facility. We have no large pharmacy."

"Other places in the Spiral Arm have those things. Rlinda Kett was just here, Olaf Reeves has visited us."

"We cut all those ties." Jeremiah's face darkened. "We have no ships of our own, and we can't just go exploring."

"We have the Klikiss transportal. We can reconnect the power source. I could travel through, find help."

"You will not. I forbid it."

Daniel was shocked. "Then you would guarantee the deaths of a third of our people."

"I guarantee nothing. God takes each one of us, and He decides the time."

"If we give up, then *we* decide the time. The storm here lasts only a few weeks, you told me so yourself. We just need to survive that long. Maybe the Roamers could evacuate us for a short while and then bring us back. It could be an easy solution, and it would prevent so much unnecessary death."

The leader raised his arm as if about to strike Daniel down. "That would be even more dangerous to our way of life, opening the doors to a contamination of a different sort."

"I'm just suggesting filter masks!" Daniel snapped. "It could save us, something so simple."

Jeremiah looked sad instead of angry. "And what happens the next time we need something easy? When someone suggests that we could feed more of our people if we accepted giant harvesting machines? What if they offered us swift transportation so we could go farther with greater convenience? Then we would die as surely as if we had perished from the spores. The neo-Amish will remain true to ourselves. That is my decision, and the people will follow me."

Daniel heaved a heavy sigh. "And is that what the upper village would say? Will those dying people all agree with you now, Father Jeremiah?"

The leader squared his shoulders and adjusted his wide-brimmed hat. "Yes, I believe so. Ever since Rickard arrived, I have been meaning to go check on them. I will travel up there and see with my own eyes. I will come back." He set his mouth in a grim line. "It will prepare me for what is in store for us here."

$$\qquad (\quad \bullet \quad)$$

The colony leader was gone for only a day, and he returned with a heavy heart and a dark report. Daniel stood close to Serene and their children, listening to him. "Twenty dead there already. They are tending their sick and burying their dead. I prayed with them, and I helped them dig new graves. I invited the healthy ones to come down with us, but they know the grieka spores will also blossom here soon. Up in the high meadows the winds are brisk and most of the spore pods have already burst. The storm will pass, and the survivors will carry on. We must do the same when it happens here."

Jeremiah's eyes were moist and red. He regarded the frightened listeners, who muttered before nodding their acceptance.

Then he sneezed and coughed. He wiped his eyes. Daniel had thought the man was crying, his eyes reddened with tears, but now he noticed the first signs of allergic swelling. Father Jeremiah had been exposed to the spores up in the meadows.

While the other neo-Amish blindly heeded Jeremiah's pronouncements, Daniel's thoughts continued to churn. He looked at his three perfect children, his beautiful wife, and thought of Happiness. Years ago, he had determined to no longer fight against his circumstances, against the neo-Amish and against his exile. But now he felt an urgency and determination. He might have the only way they could survive.

Next morning when Father Jeremiah did not come out to work in the fields, Daniel and Serene went to check on him. Serene brought the colony leader fresh bread, cheese, and coffee for his breakfast. They found Jeremiah groaning on his narrow bed. His eyes were swollen shut, oozing greenish pus.

Serene swallowed hard, but didn't rush forward in dismay. Rather she simply went to the water basin, moistened a washrag, and tended the sick man. They all knew the sequence that would happen now. Maybe he would recover, maybe he wouldn't.

Regarding the bearded leader, Daniel turned to his wife, terrified to imagine how he would feel to see her in bed like this, or his sons and daughter, trying to make them comfortable in a futile effort. "I will not let it happen," he said in a voice that was more of a growl. "Serene, tend to Father Jeremiah and watch over our children. I have someplace to go."

She looked at him in alarm, but accepted his decision. She went back to dabbing Jeremiah's sweating forehead with the wet cloth.

Stepping outside, Daniel looked across the valley where he saw the carpet of growing green grieka plants, now mottled with splashes of color, a vibrant cheerful pink. Many of the flowers were starting to bloom.

CHAPTER EIGHT

Garrison Reeves

With all the papers signed and the deal done, Garrison arranged for the sixteen prefabricated modules to be carried aboard an Iswander Industries vessel flown by Elisa Enturi. She wanted to be there in his triumphant moment when he delivered the modules to Rendezvous. The large, versatile structures could be used for habitation, industry, or even storage.

As Garrison got to know her, he found that he and Elisa had much in common. Elisa had no great love for Roamers (with the exception of Lee Iswander), considering them backward and unruly, but Garrison managed to convince her that he was also an exception, and fundamentally different from his father. In Elisa's eyes, Olaf Reeves represented everything that was wrong with the clans, and Garrison could not disagree.

"Things will change when I am clan leader after him," Garrison promised. "These modules will help us finish our grand project—a project that no other clan believed we would ever complete. That way I'll demonstrate to my father, my family, and all Roamers exactly what kind of leader I will be."

Kevin J. Anderson

He flew the *Workhorse* alongside her ship into the Meyer system, arrowing toward the asteroid cluster. Garrison felt proud, although he could not deny a flutter of anxiety. Despite his bold discussions with Elisa, he worried his father would not react well. Olaf was determined not to do anything the efficient way, the practical way, the "easy" way, because only he understood the "right" way.

Elisa maintained comm silence, while Garrison transmitted loudly on all bands. His brother Dale's face appeared on the screen. "We expected you back four days ago, Garrison. Did something happen to you?"

Garrison smiled. "Nothing happened to me, Dale. But I brought something that will save us far more than a few extra days of time—it'll change Rendezvous. We might actually see this project done in our own lifetimes."

Olaf's bearded face crowded out Dale as he brushed the younger man aside. "I'll be the judge of that. We're detecting two incoming ships. Who is with you?"

Garrison chose his words carefully. "A woman representing ... another Roamer clan." Lee Iswander was indeed a Roamer, but he knew his father wouldn't like this. "I purchased some equipment that will help our work."

The older man looked skeptical. "It's about damn time other Roamers saw their Guiding Star."

"We all do, Father," Garrison said, then signed off the comm.

As they had planned ahead of time, Elisa's ship dropped off the sixteen modules at one of the satellite asteroids just outside the main cluster. The structures floated free in space, anchored to the surface of the satellite asteroid with monofilament tethers. Led by the chief mechanic, Bjorn Elkand, ten curious members of clan Reeves arrived at the satellite asteroid. Bjorn sounded delighted when he realized the potential of the modules.

Both ships headed to the central asteroid complex, landing inside the main bay. When he and Elisa emerged from their respective vessels, Garrison was nervously smiling. Dale looked shell-shocked and silent, joined by beautiful Sendra Detemer, who had made up her mind she wanted to marry Garrison someday. Sendra's face showed a flare of jealousy when she spotted the

54

exotic Elisa Enturi traveling with him. Elisa came to stand by him, clearly satisfied with her large business deal.

Garrison strode forward. "Did you see the modules, Dale? That'll save a year's worth of work right from the outset, and we can build upon that. Once we show real progress, I can convince additional clans to chip in. We'll remake Rendezvous with an even brighter future."

The smile froze on his face when Olaf entered the chamber like a walking storm, and all hope dwindled from Garrison's heart. "What the hell do you think you're doing?"

"Thank you, Father." He felt like a fool for thinking the man would welcome any change to his grandiose plan. "This is Elisa Enturi, a representative from Iswander Industries."

"Iswander? What the—"

Garrison continued talking, intentionally ignoring his father's reaction. "With the clan Reeves line of credit, I secured these sixteen advanced modules manufactured by Iswander Industries on Earth."

"How did they get here from Earth?" Olaf demanded.

"We brought them," Elisa said in a stony voice. He realized with some embarrassment that she had expected exactly this reaction, even though she didn't even know Olaf Reeves. "Contracted and delivered. Your son came to our headquarters, negotiated with Lee Iswander to reach a mutually beneficial deal. If you wish, I can supervise the installation of these modules and instruct your clan members in their use." Her tone held cool sarcasm.

"I do not wish," Olaf growled. "And I do not wish you here. This is a Roamer place. Lee Iswander turned his back on his heritage, but you were never a Roamer at all, were you, woman?"

"No, sir. And I was never a bigot either." Her eyes flared. "I am what I've made of myself. I rose above the disadvantages and prejudices of my upbringing."

Olaf recoiled; no one had ever spoken to him like that before. Then she drove in the knife further. "I'm pleased to see Garrison is rising above his family prejudices as well. Visionary people can break free of the chains that hold them back. By bringing you these modules to improve your construction project, he's demonstrated that he will be a forward-thinking clan leader."

"We don't want your modules," Olaf said. "Take them back and return our money. We don't need any favors from Earth."

"It's not a favor—it's a business deal," Garrison said.

"It's from *Earth*!" Olaf roared. "The Earth Defense Forces destroyed Rendezvous, and I will not accept their help as a way of forgetting what they've done. Take your modules away."

"No. I refuse." Elisa crossed her arms over her breasts. "It was a business deal, duly executed by an authorized representative of clan Reeves. The modules are paid for, and I've delivered them as requested. Our business is completed."

Garrison felt furious, on Elisa's behalf as well as his own. "Father, how dare you treat her that way? The Roamer clans operate on a basis of honor."

"We—she is from Earth. She has no honor!" Olaf snapped.

"Obviously, neither do you," Elisa said. "I no longer require any further hospitality from Rendezvous. Thank you for your business, Garrison." She returned to her ship in the landing bay, leaving Olaf Reeves defiant but impotent behind her. She hadn't even entered the main complex. Now she sealed her ship behind her.

Sendra Detemer wore an amused smirk on her face, pleased to see the clan leader put in his place. Dale's expression was full of horror.

When the Iswander ship's engines roared, Elisa didn't even request clearance. She simply departed through the atmosphere-containment field and dodged away from the broken asteroids.

Olaf looked furious enough to suffer a stroke. "We will not touch those modules. They have nothing to do with us."

"Then you're a fool, Father. They are viable equipment. Roamers always make use of any available resources."

"Not resources from Earth," Olaf said. "Earth destroyed this place."

After Elisa's shocking defiance, Garrison felt his own increasing anger. "You are the one destroying this place, Father. You are not focused—you're blind."

Olaf strode over to the wall intercom and called the chief engineer. "Bjorn, withdraw your teams and cease operations with those modules. We will not use them."

Bjorn's voice came back. "But they're perfectly adequate. I've already figured out how we can expand asteroid number six. It'll allow us to reopen operations within a month, and from there we can—"

Olaf shouted into the intercom. "I issued my command! Disengage the tethers and make sure the modules drift far enough from Rendezvous that they don't pose a further navigational hazard."

The other end of the comm remained quiet for a long moment. "You certain, Olaf? It seems such a waste."

"It's for our own protection. I'm the clan leader. Do as I say." He switched off the intercom without waiting for a response.

Garrison stood simmering, so angry he couldn't speak. Olaf gave him a haughty glare, as if he had just achieved some kind of victory. Those efficient and expensive Iswander modules would soon be drifting loose, wasted, a symbol of Iswander's innovation as well as the stubborn ignorance of clan Reeves.

At the breaking point, Garrison stepped forward. "That was a stupid thing to do, Father. I'm trying to lead this clan, to show the rest of the Roamers that we aren't as foolhardy as they all say we are. Now we won't achieve success because of your stubborn arrogance."

Olaf didn't speak. He simply reached out and struck Garrison across the face, slapping him hard. Garrison stood strong, felt the pain burning on his skin, but he would not back down. His father had tried to grind him under his heel too many times, had stifled him again and again. This time, Garrison responded. He slapped his father back.

Astonished, Olaf's eyes flared wide. Dale gasped out loud.

Garrison stepped away. "Don't treat me like a fool, Father, when you're an even bigger one."

Without another word, Garrison climbed back inside the *Workhorse* and activated the engines. He felt no regrets as he flew away from Rendezvous.

CHAPTER NINE

Rlinda Kett

ith good grace, Rlinda let Tasia and Robb fly the *Voracious Curiosity* off to Newstation. Although she wouldn't admit it, she was perfectly happy to let someone else do the piloting, so long as they agreed to take care of the maintenance and paperwork once they docked at the Roamer station.

Though he was only eight years old, Xander seemed intensely interested in the controls of the piloting deck. He was no rambunctious child; rather, he seemed ready to become a pilot in a year or two.

"We're going to make a detour on our way to Newstation," Rlinda announced. When Robb looked up in surprise from the navigation console, she made a calming gesture. "It'll be less than a day. I *do* have an actual job as Trade Minister, you know. I can't just fly wherever I like."

Tasia laughed. "Shizz, I thought that's exactly what your job was."

"I suppose it is, but Peter and Estarra want me to check out the new Roamer skymining operations at Belliros. Clan Duquesne put two cloud harvesters into service, and they've been at it for six months without incident. I want to applaud them."

"We can report to Speaker Kellum, too." Tasia lounged back in the too-wide pilot's seat as Robb plotted the alternate course. "Where did clan Duquesne get the financing for two skymines? When my brother Ross built a new one he stretched our clan finances to the breaking point." She scowled. "And then the damn hydrogues blasted it out of the clouds within the first months."

"The Duquesnes aren't a wealthy family?" Robb asked.

Tasia laughed. "They don't have much money or much good will."

Rlinda drew a breath. "They got the financing to buy two mothballed skymines through a special grant from the Confederation, and in return they promised to deliver eighty percent of their production to the CDF for ten years. We need the stardrive fuel, and not many clans are willing to risk skymining again. Even though the hydrogues haven't shown themselves in nine years, we all know they're still down there, probably angry."

Robb swallowed hard. "Nobody likes angry hydrogues." He and a small group of prisoners had been held hostage deep within a gas giant, prodded and tortured by the liquid-crystal aliens as well as the evil Klikiss robots. "I hoped they were completely defeated."

"*Defeated* may just be another word for plotting revenge," Rlinda said. "I wouldn't bet my life that we've seen the last of them."

"Sounds like clan Duquesne is making exactly that bet," Tasia said.

(•)

The equatorial bands of Belliros were habitable, though frequently plagued by moon-sized storms. As the *Curiosity* approached the swirling soup of gray-green clouds, Rlinda watched several ekti tank arrays racing off.

"That's a lot of stardrive fuel," Robb said. "I thought they were supposed to sell most of it to the CDF."

Rlinda frowned as she watched the tank array depart. "That was the arrangement, but it looks like the Duquesnes made side deals as well. Good thing this is an unannounced visit. I'll have to ... mention it to them." She took the comm controls herself and contacted the primary skymine. "This is Trade Minister Rlinda Kett here for an inspection tour. I'd also like to meet with Clyde Duquesne at his earliest convenience." She switched off the voice pickup and grumbled, "And it better be convenient pretty damn soon."

The surly old clan leader was surprised to hear from her. He sputtered and made excuses, then thought better of it and welcomed them. Tasia received landing coordinates, but Rlinda took the controls. "I'll fly her in myself."

Two more ekti tank arrays darted off. The traders—black marketeers, presumably—had obviously eavesdropped on the transmissions.

The skymine was an old wreck, damaged in a hydrogue attack during the War, but it was now back in service. Rlinda landed smoothly on the designated open-air platform near the top of the control decks. As they emerged, Tasia held her son's hand. "Don't run—you might slip off the edge of the platform and then you'd fall for hours ... before the hydrogues got you."

Xander didn't seem impressed. "If I fell for hours, you'd have time to fly down and catch me before the hydrogues got me."

Robb patted the boy's shoulder. "If you were dumb enough to fall off the edge, what makes you think we'd bother to retrieve you?"

The winds whistled around the detection towers and the weather-monitoring systems. Some brave Roamers had climbed up the tall, flimsy towers, paying no attention to the heights. Others flew skimmerbikes off to raft platforms that would become satellite storage depots when clan Duquesne produced ekti faster than they could ship it to customers.

Grizzled Clyde Duquesne, wearing a faded Roamer jumpsuit and a long red scarf, strode out to meet them. In the high skies, the winds blew his thin white hair and the scarf around his face. He was accompanied by a haughty-looking young man, who sneered openly while Clyde pretended to smile. Rlinda wasn't sure which expression she preferred. Neither, she decided.

The clan leader extended a hand. "Captain Kett, we didn't expect you."

"Obviously," she muttered. "The King and Queen wanted me to check your skymining operations, and since we're heading for Newstation, I can report to Speaker Kellum about what you're doing here." She frowned. "I hope all those ekti tank arrays were headed for Earth, per your financing agreement. The military needs fuel more than anyone, so we can maintain our defenses."

"Of course." Clyde looked embarrassed. "Some of those traders were also taking samples as a goodwill gesture to other clan operations. Potential customers, in the long term."

Rlinda knew he was lying through his teeth. The young man at his side spoke up. "Roamers stick together. We have to make this business viable, in light of the risks we're taking."

"Nobody's claiming otherwise," Rlinda said. "I just prefer that people keep their agreements."

"Our second skymine will be up and running within the month," Clyde said. "And we'll double our production. My son Aaron is impatient and ambitious—good qualities in a business manager."

"So is reliability," Tasia said.

Clyde brushed her concerns aside. "Let's not dwell on the matter. I'll give you a tour of the skymine so you can make an accurate report. We're very proud of what we've accomplished."

Clyde Duquesne led them through the operations, taking them from level to level. The huge structure drifted over Belliros, skimmed the misty clouds with dangling kilometers-long probe antennae that analyzed the atmospheric composition. Wide intake scoops drew in the chemical-laden gases, and processed them through giant, roaring reactor chambers to skim out the rare hydrogen allotrope that powered stardrives.

"The chemical composition of these cloud bands is adequate for conversion to ekti." Clyde gestured toward his teams of Roamer engineers working at the monitoring stations. "The ekti potential is lower than in some gas giants, but we chose Belliros because it was relatively quiescent during the Elemental War. The drogues weren't too territorial about this world."

"Who can understand the hydrogues?" Robb asked.

Clyde Duquesne scratched the stubble on his left cheek and tossed one end of his red scarf over his shoulder. "All I understand is that we need to produce stardrive fuel, and this is our best shot. If the drogues don't bother me, then I won't bother them. We'll happily harvest ekti and be good neighbors."

"Until they come up and attack," Tasia said.

Rlinda shot her a glare. "We're not trying to discourage the Roamer operations."

"We're realistic about the danger," said Aaron, "but we decided to take the risk anyway, because the first Roamers back in ekti production will be rich."

Clyde nodded at his son. "That's what we're counting on."

For centuries, the Roamer clans had operated huge skymines on many gas giants, producing stardrive fuel for both the Terran Hanseatic League and the alien Ildiran Empire. The clans had made themselves indispensible and wealthy by becoming the primary providers of ekti—until the mysterious hydrogues had risen up in their crystalline warglobes to destroy one Roamer skymine after another, forcing the clans to stop harvesting ekti, even though humans and Ildirans were utterly dependent on the stardrive fuel. After years of the most devastating conflict in human history, the defeated hydrogues had retreated into gas giants, but the deep-core aliens were still there and could still pose a threat.

Rlinda understood the extreme risk that clan Duquesne was taking, and she didn't entirely begrudge them making a profit on the side. When the second cloud harvester went online, not only would it increase production here on Belliros, it would also prove the concept and convince other clans to get into the business again.

If only the hydrogues left them alone in the meantime.

Finished with the tour, Clyde was eager to get them back to the *Curiosity* and on their way, and Rlinda had seen all she needed to see. Standing next to the ship, they looked out at the restless sea of mists, smelling the bitter tang of chemicals as deep storms stirred the undercurrents.

The boy Xander leaned over the rail and peered down. "Will we see any hydrogues?" Robb took hold of his collar so that he wouldn't fall overboard.

"Let's hope not," Tasia said.

"We've seen no sign of them at all," Clyde said in a vehement voice.

"They won't bother us," Aaron insisted. "They got trounced so badly we'll never see their warglobes again."

"I hope you're right," Rlinda said. "I'll deliver my report to Speaker Kellum as well as to the King and Queen on Theroc. Keep doing what you're doing." She hardened her voice. "Just remember where your priorities are. The CDF needs stardrive fuel—and you'll definitely want their Mantas and Juggernauts fully fueled if the drogues ever show themselves."

"If we were in trouble, they'd never get here in time," Aaron said.

"Probably not," Clyde added, "but Captain Kett is right. If we weren't optimistic, we wouldn't have taken this deal in the first place."

"I'm sure everything will turn out just fine." Rlinda looked down at the mysterious clouds, watched air currents make dizzying swirls below. The thick clouds of Belliros could have hidden anything. "It's not just whistling past the graveyard." She fervently hoped she was right.

CHAPTER TEN

Daniel

He didn't want to go, didn't want to leave his family, but Daniel was the only one who could accomplish this mission. He knew that.

He put on clean clothes and took the better of his two hats, while Serene packed him some cheese, smoked sausage, two apples, nuts, and half a loaf of grainy bread. Then he went to say goodbye to his children. He found them playing with other boys and girls outside the schoolhouse, since the teacher had suspended classes. Daniel called out, "Ruth, Malachi, Enoch—come here!" They ran up with worried expressions, while the other boys and girls stopped playing.

"What's the pack for?" asked Malachi.

"I'm going away for a little while to see if I can bring help."

"Can I go?" asked Enoch.

Daniel's heart broke. Yes, he wanted to take them with him, all of them. He knew the doom that the colorful grieka flowers would bring. If his family followed him through the transportal wall, they would be safe from the coming spore storm—but none of the others in the community would be. These were his people now, his extended family, and he wouldn't abandon them.

"Not this time. I have to help everyone." He swept them up in a fierce embrace, feeling the solidity of their bodies. These children were his. He and Serene had created them. They were part of his heart and his blood. He had to save them. *He had to!* "Take care of your mother. Watch over her, and she'll watch over you."

Ruth started to cry, sensing how dangerous this was. Daniel pulled away, not wanting to disturb them further. "It'll be all right. I'll come back in time."

On his way out of the village, he stopped to see Serene one last time. Her hair was disheveled and moist with perspiration. She and three other women worked hard tending Jeremiah, but the colony leader had been exposed to too many toxic spores. His fever had risen, and when he coughed the burbling mucous inside his lungs was so thick he could barely take a breath.

Daniel kissed the top of her head. "I'll save us."

"You're going back there, aren't you? Father Jeremiah said you should not."

"Jeremiah is dying," he said, "and I won't let that happen to all of us."

Trembling, she pressed her face against his chest. "Will you come back?"

He drew away, startled. "Of course I will. I'm not running away."

"I know, husband, but I just worry for all of us."

"I will come back in time," he promised.

He held tighter and then released her before he changed his mind and decided just to stay and hope while a third of them died. No, he decided, that would not happen.

He left the village and headed into the hills. All around, he saw thousands of the fleshy spore flowers. The smoke from the Van Deen fires showed where they had burned their fields to stop the plants, but it was a futile gesture. There were so many of the plants ... so many.

On a hillside at the outskirts of the valley, he found the trapezoidal wall built by the Klikiss race millennia ago, the dimensional gateway that connected numerous worlds. The transportal was surrounded by coordinate tiles, each one written in the strange insect language.

After Daniel had been dumped here on Happiness, Jeremiah Huystra had deactivated the power source, disconnecting the Klikiss gateway so that no other outsiders could come through— and also making it impossible for Daniel to return to reclaim his throne. With the love of Serene and a satisfying life that was not built upon false principles, Daniel realized that he didn't want to go back, that he had no interest in riches and power. He was happy to be with these people. *His* people.

Daniel had told no one that three years ago he'd secretly come back to the Klikiss transportal and studied how Jeremiah Huystra had supposedly destroyed the alien power source. But the rigorous Klikiss technology had endured for thousands of years, and one human man with a hoe could not wreck it permanently. Daniel had managed to repair the damage done and reconnect the power source, just in case. It was easy enough, since he had, after all, been trained by OX, the Teacher compy, as well as some of the best experts in the Hansa.

Back then, when he was about to reactivate the transportal, he had hesitated, then decided to leave it be. He had gone back home. To Serene. To his three children. To his real life now.

But the transportal was always there and ready. He had not wondered about the Spiral Arm, the Hansa, or missed opportunities for many years. Now, though, he had to.

Working with a small toolkit, Daniel knelt in the soft, mossy ground. He manipulated the Klikiss circuitry, connecting power leads and reestablishing the energy flow throughout the transportal. He saw no indication that its systems were active again, but he felt a faint hum throughout the stone and he knew the system was ready ... even though he himself was not.

Daniel stared at the coordinate tiles. He didn't remember any of the symbols, did not know where they might take him, but he had to go, had to find some help. Someone would come to rescue Happiness. From the look of the spore flowers, the colony had maybe a week before the buds burst and spread their spores throughout the valley.

He swallowed hard. Rlinda Kett and Olaf Reeves had filled them in on the political situation out in the Spiral Arm, and the Confederation seemed to be at peace. He was sure he could find help. Someone would provide the filters, technology, and medical assistance they needed.

He selected a coordinate tile at random, one whose design looked pleasing to him. As the alien network activated, he watched the flat stone surface shimmer and open up to reveal the other side of the gateway. A new planet. He saw structures, *human* structures—small outbuildings, a control shack, new dwellings. This was it, a good opportunity. These people could point him in the right direction.

Daniel stepped through, terrified of what he would find and the decisions he would have to face. But he had no doubts. He had to do this.

CHAPTER ELEVEN

Olaf Reeves

For days after Garrison stormed away, Olaf could still feel the sting in his cheek from where his son—his own son!—had struck him. It was disrespectful and deeply unsettling. His fists clenched, and he did not know how to respond. He tried not to let rage dictate his actions, because he was not a man who made his decisions based on anger, but rather on determination and clarity of purpose. His Guiding Star.

Bjorn transmitted to the main asteroid complex. "All those modules are cut loose and dispersed, by your orders, Olaf. They're adrift far enough from the other asteroids that they won't pose any problems." The engineer fell silent for a long tense moment, then added, "It's a damn shame, all those perfectly good resources...."

"We'll do fine without them," Olaf said. "Doing business with Earth might have gained us a few years, but would cost our souls."

Bjorn clearly did not agree, but didn't contradict him on the open comm.

Olaf went back to his office and mulled over what to do next. Finally he summoned his other son—perhaps his only son now. "I need to see you, Dale. We have important matters to discuss."

"I'll be there in just a minute, Father." He knew Dale would practically run, so as not to displease him. Dale was so different from his brother....

Garrison had his little tantrum, but Olaf wondered if it was more than that. They had had arguments before, increasingly contentious disputes about the future of clan Reeves. Yes, he was allowed to express other ideas, but the clan leader had the final say, and everyone needed to accept that. Garrison didn't understand the proper hierarchy.

Olaf had been opinionated and argumentative with his own father back when he was young, long before the Elemental War, but that rebellious phase had been brought sharply under control. He doubted that Garrison's problem would be resolved so cleanly.

Now that several days had passed, a heavy feeling hardened in the pit of his stomach, replacing the anger. He expected his son to return, contrite, to beg forgiveness. But after such a sharp confrontation, Olaf knew it might take days or weeks for the young man to make up his mind and apologize. But Olaf feared there was something different this time, something worse.

What if Garrison never came back? What if he went with that woman instead?

Flushed from running, Dale arrived in the admin office and stood before his father's desk, looking anxious. He was a thin young man with pale skin, a long face, and large eyes that gave him a rabbitty appearance. Olaf didn't rise, nor did he give Dale the opportunity to sit. "You and I need to discuss possible changes in clan Reeves."

Dale blinked. "Changes? Shouldn't we wait for Garrison?"

"I'm done waiting for Garrison to accept his role as the next clan leader. Therefore, provisionally, I rescind that title from him." Dale gasped, and Olaf continued. "I have no choice but to consider you to be the future of clan Reeves."

"I ... think you're overreacting, Father. Emotions are high. You both have tempers." He swallowed hard. "I'm sorry, but it's true. Garrison has his Guiding Star, and he did what he thought best for the clan and for Rendezvous."

Olaf forced himself to remain seated behind the desk. "You're defending him?"

Dale swallowed. "Those modules would have been a big help here, and you just discarded them."

Olaf sighed. "I can see I have to teach better priorities to our people here."

When Dale's shoulders sagged, Olaf knew he had won the point.

Around the admin office—once the Roamer Speaker's office, back in the glory days of Rendezvous—he had placed historical images of the thriving asteroid complex, the artificial habitats, the numerous domes and connecting tubes. Images showed countless designs of Roamer ships patched together from other components, modifications created either by inspiration or necessity. Olaf liked to admire them, a display of the best Roamer abilities.

He activated controls on his desk to project a hologram that drew Dale's attention. "Rendezvous, as it can be again," Olaf said in a low voice filled with awe. "This is what we had. This is what the Roamer clans built, and this is what we must recreate. That task falls to us, since the other Roamers have lost sight of the true goal." The shimmering hologram showed the precise arrangement of drifting rocks, connecting structures, and outlying facilities from before the attack from the Earth military.

Alas, it would not be possible to rebuild the asteroid complex exactly, because the EDF had destroyed some of the orbiting rocks, but Olaf intended to reassemble the debris as perfectly as possible, even if everyone else lost interest.

Looking at his son, he sighed. "I've concluded, Dale, that this lack of drive is my own failing. I let Garrison address the clans about our dream, and he just proved that his heart is not in it. Therefore, it's time for me to go to the Confederation myself." Now he rose from his desk and stood over the slowly rotating image of the asteroid complex. "The King and Queen need to understand what we once had. Just because Roamers joined the Confederation doesn't mean we must give up our independence and our culture."

"Of course not," Dale said. "That was explicitly stated in the charter."

"Nevertheless, they need to be reminded," Olaf said in a sharper voice. "I've talked to our clan leaders to the point of oxygen deprivation, but I'll go to Theroc and maybe Peter and Estarra will show their support for our dream." He sighed. "And if they don't, then we'll do it ourselves, as I always vowed to do."

"Should I go with you, Father? Be at your side?"

"No, I'll take Bjorn. I am leaving you here to supervise the reconstruction. You'll need to take on more duties like that if you're to be clan leader someday. I'll instruct the clan members to follow your directives."

"Yes, Father." Dale seemed far out of his depth, and Olaf knew he would have to be hard on his younger son to mold him into the necessary personality. The role should have fallen to Garrison, but that was not to be.

Olaf clenched his hands again as he felt his dream slipping through his fingers. He needed to hold everything together to make Rendezvous what it should be. Through sheer force of will, he could make this project happen.

He held back a sigh, thinking of Garrison and that woman, Elisa Enturi. He thought of how Lee Iswander had given up his principles, yet still pretended to call himself a Roamer ... and he thought of the Earth Defense Forces, everyone who had caused so much damage. Olaf could trust only his sadly dwindling number of followers, because only they could see the proper Guiding Star.

Maybe it was too much, too difficult. Maybe it would be best if he and the remaining members of clan Reeves just isolated themselves, found someplace to be self-sufficient and live on their own terms, as the neo-Amish had done on Happiness.

But Olaf wasn't ready to do that. Not yet. But perhaps soon ...

CHAPTER TWELVE

Rlinda Kett

After leaving the clan Duquesne skymines, Rlinda was impressed to see the busy Roamer complex of Newstation. The clans had pooled their resources and their energy to construct a gigantic new operations center from scratch.

The huge old-school space station was a rotating wheel with centripetal force creating artificial gravity. Seven spokes radiated out to the rim from a central complex at the hub. Commercial spaceships flitted about, transporting people and materials, but over half of the vessels were construction ships. Three quarters of the wheel space station had been completed, and the rest of the framework already defined the ring.

Rlinda shook her head in amazement. "Ten years ago the Roamers were scattered outlaws. I'd say they made quite a comeback."

Tasia admired the station as she flew the *Voracious Curiosity* closer. "There's no stopping Roamer clans once they get a big idea in their heads."

After visiting Olaf Reeves's faltering project at Rendezvous, Rlinda had read up on the new Roamer complex as well. While

Rendezvous had been built centuries ago as an accidental waystop, the site of Newstation had been a carefully considered choice. The Roamers selected an otherwise-uninhabited planet, Auridia, which had a Klikiss transportal and thus served as a nexus point for travelers using the interdimensional gateways. Auridia was conveniently located among heavily populated systems in the Confederation and not far from the Ildiran Empire. Speaker Del Kellum had selected this as the best spot for a new government center.

The Roamers chose to build their main complex in orbit, though, so their ships did not need to land and take off from the planet's gravity well with each visit. Roamers were not planetbound. They liked to fly their own ships, rather than use Klikiss transportals.

Robb opened up the comm. "This is the *Voracious Curiosity* bearing the Confederation's Trade Minister—if such things impress you. Do you have a docking bay for us?"

With a huff, Rlinda took over the comm. "And we're also being piloted by Tasia Tamblyn, if that gains us any more favors among the Roamers."

The traffic operator laughed. "We're impressed enough with both the Trade Minister and a member of clan Tamblyn. Jess Tamblyn is here along with Cesca Peroni. You're here to see them?"

"It's on our list of things to do," Tasia said.

A glittering pockmarked ice ball hung near the rotating station, a wandering comet that had been diverted here. The Roamers excavated the ice for water, oxygen, and standard rocket fuel, but Rlinda saw that the comet was suffused with an eerie glow. She knew what it meant. "Jess and Cesca brought the wentals there, didn't they?"

"Yes, but the water elementals have been diminished," Tasia said. "Their power isn't fatal anymore."

"Good thing," Robb said, "if they want to turn the hollow comet into a school for Roamer children."

Xander came forward to the piloting deck, watching all the activity. He focused on the glowing comet. "Will I have to go to school there?"

"Maybe we'll *let* you go to school there," Robb teased. "Only the best Roamer children will be selected."

"Then I'll be one of the best Roamer children," Xander said.

"You already are," Tasia said. "Because we raised you right."

Flying through the flurry of Roamer ships, she zipped down to dodge an in-system tug hauling asteroid chunks to a satellite smelter facility. At the other end of the smelter, fabrication bays shipped out thousands of square hull plates that workers towed toward the incomplete section of the Newstation torus.

After docking the *Curiosity*, they were greeted by several Roamers in traditional jumpsuits embroidered with clan symbols. A young man, so tall and thin he had apparently grown up under very low gravity, spoke quickly. "The Speaker would like to see you as soon as it's convenient, Captain Kett. He's always ready for a briefing from the Trade Minister, and I suppose he probably wants to air a few grievances."

"And he thinks I can solve them?" Rlinda asked.

The gangly young man laughed. "No, he just likes to air grievances. It might not even be about anything to do with the Confederation." He turned to Tasia and Robb as their son stood between them, drinking in the activity. "Oh, and we've set up quarters for you, compliments of the Speaker. Meanwhile, Jess and Cesca are shuttling over from the comet."

"I look forward to seeing my brother," Tasia said, "but we want to get back in touch with a lot of clan members."

"We're pilots for Kett Shipping now," Robb pointed out. "It's good to maintain contacts."

Letting the others settle in, Rlinda followed the gangly man, who escorted her to the Speaker's office. She intended to finish her business quickly, then inquire about the best restaurants aboard Newstation. As she entered his office, Rlinda said, "Del Kellum, you must not be very busy as Speaker if you can arrange a meeting with me the moment I arrive."

The big bearded man had a potbelly, a good humor, and a loud voice, much like her own. "I was so anxious to see you, I wanted to keep my schedule fluid. Did King Peter send you here on an urgent mission? Is the Spiral Arm under grave threat again?"

She smiled and took the seat he offered. "As far as I know, the fate of the universe isn't at stake this week. Believe it or not, this is just a social visit—classified as business, or course. But you and I can hash out some trade negotiations, open a few routes to your clans, reserve other routes for Kett Shipping. Make sure the Confederation is running smoothly."

"Smoothly enough." Del reached into his embedded desk drawer and withdrew a small bottle, then fished out two crystal cordial glasses. "Since you're known for your fine taste in food and wines, I want you to sample my orange liqueur. Special family recipe, made by my own hands."

She took the glass he offered. "Then your schedule really is fluid if you have time to distill liqueur."

He sipped and sighed. "One must make time for important things."

Rlinda was pleased with the sweet warmth as it burned her lips and tongue. "I have to say, I'm impressed with Newstation," she said after taking another sip of orange liqueur. "Before coming here, I stopped by the old Rendezvous site to see their progress."

Kellum snorted. "I wish that stubborn old man would realize that we're all pulling together here. He's got his head stuck in the past, but the rest of us have moved on."

"I doubt he'll ever admit that, Speaker Kellum."

Kellum refilled their glasses and raised his in a toast. "I think you're right, Captain Kett."

"I'm right about a lot of things. Now, let's get to the trade negotiations."

On her pad, she called up her list of ships, the star map of Confederation planets as well as runs to the Ildiran Empire. Rlinda also delivered her report about clan Duquesne and their skymining work on Belliros. "So far, so good," she said. "Maybe other clans will take a chance and get back into skymining."

"Still no sign of the hydrogues?" Del asked.

"No sign. Everything quiet and peaceful." *Like a graveyard*, she thought.

☾   •   ☽

After making her well-considered dinner plans, she made her way back to her quarters and found that Tasia and Robb's suite was open across the hall. Jess Tamblyn and Cesca Peroni were inside, chatting with the others.

Cesca had been the Speaker for the Roamer clans during the height of the Elemental War. She and Jess had both been infused with the deadly power of the wentals, but that force was drained out of them, and now they had come here, where they intended to devote their efforts to teaching children.

"The comet school is going to be called Academ," Jess said. "The excavations already stripped out a lot of the viable ices, leaving empty tunnels and chambers."

Tasia turned to Rlinda and announced, "We're going to stay here at Newstation awhile and work with my brother inside the comet. Gotta make sure it's an appropriate school for Xander."

"I won't mind flying the *Curiosity* myself again," Rlinda said, then turned back to her own quarters. "Keep talking for as long as you like. Speaker Kellum is meeting me at the most expensive restaurant aboard Newstation." She crossed her beefy arms over her chest. "I warned him I'm hard to impress when it comes to fine dining, and I hope he surprises me."

Her stomach growled in anticipation, and the others laughed. After so many years of stress, she was glad the human race could build a new golden age, unharrassed by primal forces that intended to kill them.

Yes, times were good. She just wished BeBob could be here with her.

CHAPTER THIRTEEN

Elisa Enturi

As they surreptitiously returned to the Meyer system, Elisa rode with Garrison in the *Workhorse*. The blood-red dwarf star looked like an angry eye.

In the pilot seat, Garrison tried to appear relaxed, but she could tell he was tense. "Coming in on this vector, we'll stay behind Meyer. Rendezvous won't detect our arrival, so we can take our time to scan for those drifting modules."

Elisa shook her head. "That was perfectly serviceable equipment. Only a fool would have discarded them because of pride or stupidity."

"My father is a stubborn fool," Garrison said without even a hint of a smile. "That's not an opinion; he's proved it again and again."

She had wanted to take an Iswander Industries' ship to locate and retrieve the drifting modules, but Garrison insisted that the *Workhorse* had all the necessary ID codes as well as the detailed navigational paths in and around the asteroid cluster. Elisa had agreed for her own reasons, knowing that if she signed out a company vessel, there would have been documentation left behind, paperwork to fill out. This way was cleaner.

Garrison wanted to help her get those modules back—modules already paid for with clan Reeves funding, modules that Olaf Reeves had just thrown away. He would be too proud to ask for a refund of the money, and that worked to Elisa's advantage. If she and Garrison could retrieve them, she could surreptitiously place the modules back into service and sell them to other customers.

After leaving here several days ago, she had been furious with Olaf, and she hadn't thought much more about Garrison, dismissing him along with his Luddite family. Yes, she had found the young man intriguing, and his stories about clan activities were unsettling but exotic.

Olaf Reeves, though, was a real piece of work, the antithesis of everything Lee Iswander stood for in trying to modernize the clans and bring them in as a lucrative and influential part of the Confederation. Clan Reeves wanted to crawl back under a rock—literally. Olaf didn't deserve Iswander's modules, didn't deserve the tools that civilized people had to offer.

She and Garrison would sneak in and take them back.

Not long after she had flown back home to Earth, Garrison had found her again in the same bar, sipping another glass of the expensive New Portugal wine. He spotted her like a targeting computer locking its sights, and he came over, his face filled with grim determination as well as an expectation of shared camaraderie. His anger and annoyance had not diminished.

She had taken a sip and waited for him, raising her eyebrows. "I thought your father would lock you in your room and punish you with extra chores."

"My father locked me up in many ways, but I left Rendezvous and clan Reeves." He sighed. "I have to look forward, and my father's dreams are all backward."

She gave him a smile. "In that case, I'll buy the drinks this time."

That night, they had concocted the scheme to retrieve the perfectly intact modules Olaf had discarded at Rendezvous. "Are you sure he wasn't just blowing off steam? Trying to make a point?" Elisa asked. "After we left, he could have changed his mind and put them to use."

"Never," Garrison said. "He wouldn't let his fingers be soiled by technology from Earth, and he certainly wouldn't make life easier for his clan members, even though they supposedly share his dream."

"So those expensive modules will just keep drifting around the asteroid belt like wreckage?"

Garrison had leaned forward, sliding the wine glass aside. "No, because we're going to go retrieve them—you and I. I know how to find them."

She was intrigued. "Why would you do that?"

He put his elbows on the table. "Because then your Mr. Iswander will see that I've got worthwhile skills, and he'll find something else for me to do."

Elisa considered. "Maybe he will at that."

When the *Workhorse* arrived in the remote location, Elisa studied scans of the rubble dispersed around the dull red star. "This system has absolutely nothing of interest. Why would Roamers bother with a bunch of rocks when there are so many other planets to colonize?"

"Our ancestors were aboard the generation ship *Kanaka*, which left Earth with all the others three hundred and fifty years ago. After traveling aimlessly for more than a century, Meyer was the first system the *Kanaka* reached—and it was this place or nothing."

"Quite a disappointment, I would imagine," Elisa said.

"We tried to make the best of it. Some of the colonists established a foothold here in the asteroids, while the *Kanaka* set off again and kept searching. This was before we had the Ildiran stardrive. Roamers have always learned to make do." He turned to her. "But I'm tired of making do. Let's make some success."

"You and I think along the same lines," she said.

As the clunky *Workhorse* eased its way toward the asteroid cluster, Garrison plotted possible trajectories for the likeliest places where the modules would have wandered. He only needed two tries.

"I see them." He zoomed in on a group of reflective shapes that were too geometrical to be natural rocks. "They're still drifting together."

"Then it'll be easy," she said. "The collapsed modules can fit in the auxiliary cargo compartments of the *Workhorse*, and we'll haul them out of here."

"Not quite so simple as that," he said. "We still have to retrieve them—and keep our heads down so the others don't see us."

Elisa kept a wary eye on all the bright clan Reeves ships working in the main part of the cluster. The discarded modules had drifted far enough that they were distant from the central operations.

Shutting down his engines and running lights, Garrison went to the back compartment where he began donning the components of his exosuit. Elisa watched him move with easy habit, but she wasn't sure how to help him check the seals. "You're going out there yourself to round them up?" she asked.

He looked at her in surprise. "Of course. How else do we get them?"

"I thought the *Workhorse* had grappler arms or something."

"It's much easier to do it myself, with my own hands." His expression suddenly changed. "Oh, you're not accustomed to working outside in space!"

"No, never done it."

He laughed. "I've spent half of my time in a suit since I was ten years old. He finished placing his chest plate and attaching the life-support pack.

"Then I suppose you know what you're doing. Is there anything I can do to help?"

"Stay inside and man the comm and the piloting controls. Hold us in position." Garrison gave her another encouraging smile, then attached his helmet. "I think that's all, if you're not used to working in a suit."

After he cycled through the airlock, she returned to the control deck and watched him jet around outside. The dim red sun offered little illumination, but she could see his suit lights. When he found the modules, he activated locators so she could track them. Working alone, he clipped tethers and nudged the large packages back toward the *Workhorse*. As the collapsed modules drifted closer, he swooped in and opened the lower cargo bay to guide them inside one at a time.

She was amazed to watch Garrison work out in the vacuum with as much ease as if he had been swimming in a pool or walking through a park. In less than an hour, he had loaded one module after another, bringing all sixteen aboard the cargo bay.

Elisa felt a great sense of satisfaction, knowing these modules would go back on the Iswander account, and her boss would certainly be happy. She was about to begin the test run of her prototype sky hotel, Cloud Nine. Four surplus modules just like these had already been shipped off to Qhardin, along with the assembly crew. As soon as she returned from this errand, she would lead her first four volunteer guests to Cloud Nine. If the idea worked, she could build more sky hotels, an entirely separate income stream for Iswander Industries....

Finished, Garrison cycled back through the airlock. He removed his helmet and began to decouple the components, leaving only the slick form-fitting black singlesuit that he wore underneath. "See, I told you it could be done."

"That was easier than I thought," she said.

Garrison used a small polymer towel to scrub his damp hair and wipe perspiration off his face and neck. "That isn't often the case."

Unexpectedly, the *Workhorse*'s comm chimed an alert, and the thin face of young Dale Reeves appeared on the screen. "Attention, unidentified ship. Please state your intentions."

Garrison glanced at Elisa. "I hoped no one would spot us."

Dale continued, "This is a Roamer complex, and we will defend ourselves."

With a flicker of obvious dread, Garrison went to the screen. "Would you defend yourself against your own brother, Dale? I have no doubt that's what Father would tell you to do."

The other man looked surprised. "He left me in charge. I told him you'd come back, and now you're here, skulking around. I know he can be obstinate, but let's talk this out."

Garrison's face darkened. "I don't think so, Dale. You heard him, you saw what he did. He's a fool, locked in his personal orbit. I don't believe his decisions are best for our clan, but I won't try to overthrow him as clan leader. I've had enough. I've got my own life to live. Put him on, and I'll tell him myself."

"He's not here. He and Bjorn went off to Theroc to plead his case with the King and Queen." Dale's voice took on an odd tone. "But if you go, you'll be leaving me here with him. He intends to train me for your position as clan leader. I don't want that, Garrison!"

"Neither did I," he said, then straightened. "We're just here retrieving the modules—equipment already paid for, but our father discarded them. I'm still Roamer enough to know that you don't leave viable salvage drifting in space for someone else to find. Elisa and I are taking them back to Iswander Industries." He swallowed hard and then leaned closer to the screen. "He's grinding you under his heel, Dale. He'll destroy you if you stay too long. Come with us. We'll both find a job at Iswander Industries. You've got many Roamer skills."

Elisa could see that the younger man was far too weak to stand up for himself. In fact, Dale looked panicked by the suggestion. "This is my clan, my family ... my home. We'll rebuild Rendezvous, you'll see."

Garrison sighed. "Then I wish you the best of luck. I have to follow my own Guiding Star." He terminated the transmission before his brother could plead with him further.

Elisa looked over at him. She still wasn't sure she trusted him entirely, but he had demonstrated exceptional skills as a worker. He had many talents.

"Let's get the hell out of here." Garrison activated the *Workhorse*'s engines away from the Meyer system, turning his back on Rendezvous.

CHAPTER FOURTEEN

Daniel

The last time he'd passed through a Klikiss transportal, Daniel had been groggy, after Peter and Estarra stunned him and dumped him on a far-off planet just to get him away from the clutches of Chairman Wenceslas. This time, Daniel stepped through the shimmering wall of his own volition. It was his choice—his desperation. He had to save his people.

He felt a jarring dimensional twist through his mind and his bones. One instant he was on the moist, lush hillside, and the next he was in dry, cool air. The scenery was brown and barren, with few patches of dry grass. He stood on a concrete apron with eight small prefab outbuildings nearby. This was a tiny complex, but at least there were people. He saw three workers in jumpsuits kneeling in the dirt, planting vegetables in a small garden. A tall, heavyset woman tinkered with the engines on an overland flier.

They looked up as Daniel stepped through the transportal. He paused to catch a breath, smelling the distinctively different tang in the air, a powdery sourness from blown dust. He adjusted his wide-brimmed cap and raised a hand as he hurried forward. "I need help! I have urgent business with King Peter."

The men in the garden stood, and the woman glanced up from the disassembled flier. They looked at him curiously. No one seemed in a rush.

Daniel ran toward them. "Can't you hear me? I need help."

That finally got their attention. One of the men with his knees and hands covered in mud from the garden plot, wiped his palms on his thighs. "Who are you? Where did you come from?"

"I came from Happiness," he said. "You wouldn't know it. We've been off the network for some time. I'm Daniel." He drew a breath, swallowed hard, but he knew what he had to do. "You might know me as Prince Daniel, from the Hansa."

"The Hansa?" said the female mechanic. "Ain't been no Hansa for nine years."

"Then you know how long I've been gone," Daniel said. "My people are in trouble. I have to get to King Peter and Queen Estarra. They'll know who I am. I need to request assistance from the Confederation."

"So, what kind of clothes are those?" said one of the other men from the garden. These people didn't seem to understand urgency. Hearing the noise outside, two more workers emerged from a small administration building, and a larger metal-walled warehouse.

Daniel looked at them, saw that all of the men were clean-shaven. He touched his thick beard, the long hair that curled down to his shoulders. He hadn't shaved in several years, and Serene only occasionally trimmed his hair. He realized his floppy hat and simple clothes must give him a peculiar appearance. "I know I must look odd to you. Happiness was settled by the neo-Amish—these are their ways."

"Do you even know where you are?" asked the flier mechanic.

"I know I have to get to Theroc. I need to speak to the King and Queen as soon as possible. Can you help me?"

"You're on Auridia, young man, and the Roamer complex of Newstation orbits above us. As far as getting to Theroc, I can shuttle you up to the station, pass along your message. Speaker Kellum will find somebody to take you to Theroc straightaway."

Daniel looked up into the sky. "That'll do. When can we leave?" His heart pounded. With every moment, more sporeflower pods would burst, spraying the toxic powder into the air.

The female mechanic shrugged. "Our shuttle is fueled, and I'm always looking for an opportunity to fly. I'll take you right now. My name is Yankton, by the way." She looked around to the others at the outpost. "If you have a shopping list for me, get it together right away. This young man looks anxious."

"Looks like he needs a haircut and a bath," said the man who, ironically, was covered with mud from the garden.

Yankton gestured to a battered shuttlecraft that sat in a paved landing area a hundred meters from the transportal wall. "Get yourself aboard."

"I appreciate the effort," Daniel said to the pilot. When he'd vanished from the Hansa, the Roamers were outlaws led by Speaker Cesca Peroni. "Do you think somebody will help?" he asked in a small voice.

"Roamers like to help," she said. "Don't worry, we'll get you what you need."

☾ • ☽

Having been among the low-tech neo-Amish for so long, Daniel held on as the shuttle rose into the sky. The seats rattled and rumbled, but Yankton casually leaned back, letting one arm dangle over the armrest while she piloted with one hand. When the veils of clouds cleared away and the atmosphere thinned to midnight-blue darkness at the edge of orbit, he looked at the stars unhindered by sky. Out there, he spotted the flurry of traffic, the glitter of engine burns, as well as the huge wheel of a space station. "Roamers built that?"

The pilot shrugged. "Roamers always build big things, but other people tend to underestimate us."

When Yankton docked at an available bay in Newstation, she called for a welcoming committee. Daniel's urgent request had already been sounded throughout the station, and clan members were discussing a solution. Daniel hoped they had something for him as soon as the shuttle arrived.

They did.

Since he had traveled through the Klikiss transportal and left Happiness behind, Daniel was astonished to recognize Rlinda Kett standing there to greet him with her hands planted on her wide hips. Another man, Speaker Del Kellum, waited next to her. "It's not often we welcome a former Hansa Prince ... not that we ever had good experiences with the Hansa, by damn," Kellum said.

Rlinda shot a quick, sharp glance at the Speaker. "Past history isn't his fault, Del. He's a reasonably good kid, and I didn't think he'd ever be pried loose from his quiet peaceful existence unless he had a good reason. Did you miss my company, Daniel?"

He thanked the pilot as he stepped away from the shuttle, but Yankton was already brushing herself off and ready to take care of her own business aboard Newstation.

Daniel faced Rlinda and the Speaker. "I came because I had to. Captain Kett, you saw the home we made on Happiness. I wouldn't come here unless it was a dire urgency. I need someone to take me to Theroc. If I don't see the King and Queen, all my people are going to die."

"Die? What happened, dear boy?"

"Spore storms, a cyclical infestation." He clasped his hands together. "Please, Captain Kett—if your ship is here, can we go to Theroc? I don't have much time."

She glanced at Speaker Kellum and said, "I'll take him. Tasia and Robb are staying here for a while."

"Your ship's already refueled and prepared, compliments of the Roamer clans," Kellum said. "Be sure to put in a good word with King Peter."

"I will." Rlinda took Daniel by the arm. "I know you didn't want to see the Confederation, but we'll make this as quick and easy as we can."

Daniel's knees felt weak with relief, but he didn't show it. He just followed her at a fast pace toward the *Voracious Curiosity*.

CHAPTER FIFTEEN

Elisa Enturi

She had decided to name the first sky hotel "Cloud Nine." Her marketing instincts told her it was a name that would do well.

Elisa had used Iswander's standard authorization signature to arrange a luxury transport from Earth, and now she arrived at Qhardin with her first group of invited guests. The gas giant looked beautiful and dramatic—perfect for Elisa's purposes. The clouds were burnt orange and yellow, with darker bands of red that defined the edges of immense storms.

"Will we see hydrogues?" asked the most eager passenger, a man in his mid-twenties named Fourth, short for Charles Quinton Ruiz IV, a spoiled young son of a wealthy family. Fourth was mildly handsome, made more attractive by the size of his trust fund, and he fancied himself a playboy although he wasn't good at it. Fourth spent his days doing little of note other than amusing himself.

Elisa didn't like him. In fact, she despised people who had a sense of entitlement yet contributed nothing worthwhile to society. Her own family had been poor and unambitious, and their low economic status was their own fault, but many rich families had similarly worthless children. Nevertheless, she had selected Charles Quentin Ruiz IV as a perfect example of a demographic to which the Iswander sky hotels would cater.

Hearing the young man's query about hydrogues, the other three passengers crowded close to the viewing window. Elisa said, "I cannot guarantee it, nor can I guarantee that we won't. Rest assured that we have safety systems in place for Cloud Nine."

Elisa didn't elaborate. Her "safety systems" aboard the floating hotel modules amounted to little more than hoping that the deep-core aliens wouldn't show themselves. The hydrogues had been quiet for nearly a decade, and she knew that a couple of large Roamer skymines had been harvesting ekti from another gas giant without being molested. She assumed that her four drifting modules would easily go unnoticed.

"The drogues are down there," growled Roland Kipps, a middle-aged man with a waxy scar across his left cheek and a bald patch on the same side of his head, the result of burns he had suffered in an explosion eleven years ago. "We have to watch out for them. Those bastards might be defeated, but who knows how long they'll remember."

Kipps had survived a hydrogue attack, when the crystalline alien warglobes had leveled his colony on Ubor Major. He had been rescued from the wreckage two days later when EDF ships finally responded to the distress calls. His entire family had been killed. Kipps was one of sixteen survivors out of a colony of six thousand.

"You know better than anyone else how dangerous the hydrogues are, Mr. Kipps," said Candeen, one of the remaining two passengers. "Why would you want to come back?"

Juvia, Candeen's romantic and business partner, added, "If I'd gone through what you survived, I'd check gas giants off my bucket list forever."

The Iswander luxury ship cruised into the upper atmospheric banks, and the clouds thickened around them. Kipps had an odd look in his eyes as he stared out the windowport. "If I kept myself safe on some isolated colony, my life would be an unending sequence of nightmares. I want to stare them down. This way, once I go home maybe I'll get some peace."

There were a great many shell-shocked survivors of the War, people like Roland Kipps, and she hoped to cater to such clientele with her sky hotels. Elisa said, "We are aware that hydrogues are likely down in Qhardin's atmosphere, but we will monitor and we will remain prepared. Safety first."

She had written up an entire action plan to be implemented in due course after this proof-of-concept visit. For now, though, everything was just a test run. She wanted to prove to Mr. Iswander that this entire commercial venture was viable.

"It's like swimming in a cage with predator fish," said Juvia. "You know the danger's there, but you're fascinated by it as long as you know in your gut that you're safe."

"Mostly safe," Fourth added.

"Exactly the point," Elisa said.

Candeen slid an arm around her partner's waist during the approach to the drifting Cloud Nine modular hotel. "As long as we prove it's a good investment."

The two had matching spiral tattoos on their foreheads. Both had come from Ulio Station, a trading complex on the far side of the Confederation, which serviced Roamers, scavengers, black-marketeers, and ambitious traders. Candeen and Juvia had come upon a windfall after selling a large recovered ship to the salvage yard, and they were curious about investing in the new sky hotel idea.

The pilot of the luxury ship announced over the intercom, "We're coming in for a landing. The balcony observation platform looks a little small, but I'm sure I can fit."

"The design specs were large enough to accommodate a vessel this size," Elisa said, then looked at the passengers. "We'll expand eventually. This is just a prototype."

"But still ambitious," Juvia said.

Skimming just above the clouds, where vapors curled up to catch the slanted sunlight, four of Iswander's standard prefab modules had been connected by their mutual ports. The hotel complex could be easily expanded with a dozen or even a hundred more modules. As she saw their beautiful observation ceilings, the angled walls, the reinforced support layers, and the levitation engines underneath the clusters, she thought about how such modules could have been used at Rendezvous, if Olaf Reeves hadn't been such an ass.

The luxury ship touched down on the platform, and Elisa stepped out onto the egress ramp. The winds of Qhardin whistled in, and her ears popped, adjusting to the air pressure.

The four passengers crowded behind her, peering out at the undulating sea of restless clouds. The atmospheric vapors brought a sulfurous tang and a sickly sweet odor.

Fourth stepped out into the open. "It stinks here."

"Those chemical mixtures are what made skymining so profitable," Elisa said, hiding any sign of her annoyance.

Roland Kipps stood on the platform, his shoulders squared, his arms slightly bent at his sides. He didn't say a word as he looked around, watching the cloud banks and waiting for some monster to lunge out. Candeen and Juvia stood together, sniffing the breezes and bracing themselves against the chill. Juvia shivered. "I suppose this won't be a lounge deck then for soaking up sunshine and mineral fumes?"

Candeen chuckled.

Elisa said, "There are warmer cloud bands, and this hotel is mobile. Later I'll take you out in our skybus to tour the clouds."

"I'm anxious to get out there," said Fourth with a snort. "We don't have to relax for too long. The hotel modules don't look much bigger than the ship we just rode in."

Elisa tried to be reassuring as she pointed out for the fifth time, "This is just a 'soft' grand opening, so you'll have to put up with a few rough edges. Don't expect all the amenities that Cloud Nine will eventually have to offer. Your input will help us make the facility better for the next wave of guests."

Being crisp and polite was very hard.

Once they cycled into the central module, the four visitors were met by two dusky-skinned and dark-haired young men, Anil and Shar. Elisa had found the brothers' resumes among the Iswander employee files on Earth, and they had jumped at the chance to come to the new sky hotel as service staff on promise of guaranteed and substantial advancement if the test run proved viable.

She introduced them. "Anil and Shar will take care of your luggage, show you to your rooms, and let you relax for an hour or two. Meanwhile, I'll meet with our chief engineer, Mr. Delkin, and make sure everything's in order for a fine stay."

The two brothers helped unload the luggage from the luxury transport, and showed the guests to their three separate rooms. Elisa let out a sigh after they split up and wandered to their quarters, glad to be alone.

It was hard work for her to be sociable and gracious. Normally, Elisa liked her conversations to be on point, stating facts and doing duties. She had never been good at light banter or building relationships. Such things took too long and required too much personal effort. She preferred tasks that were cut and dried.

But she would make the effort for Lee Iswander's sake. Spending time with Garrison Reeves had recently softened her, and she felt more personable, more hopeful. She was determined to make this work.

The central module also had the mechanic's deck, with life-support equipment, power blocks and control room, as well as the community area and dining hall for the guests. In an eventual expansion, there would be a complete lobby and recreation module, and another entire admin and engineering module. She was already making plans.

In the mechanic's deck, she met Oni Delkin, whom she had hand-picked as the Cloud Nine engineer, primarily because he was immediately available, not because he was especially competent. Elisa understood the situation. Any Iswander engineer with impeccable credentials and competence would be in high demand, and she needed someone the company could live without for a week or two.

Delkin was reclining in a chair at the control decks, staring at screens that didn't seem to change much. She startled him. "Are systems online and at optimal levels?"

The man was a decade from retirement with a solid, if unremarkable, Iswander Industries career under his belt. "I've checked the diagnostic levels. All the pieces fit together, Tab A into Slot B. It seems simple enough." He shrugged. "No complications."

Elisa nodded. "That's exactly how Iswander modules are supposed to be—self-sufficient, easily erected, easily expanded."

"Yes, designed to be assembled even by idiots. And our Cloud Nine life-support systems are off-the-shelf components. We've got nothing to worry about." He laced his fingers behind his head and leaned back farther in his chair. "It'll be good to have some company and conversation, though. Those two brothers have been driving me crazy, trying to take care of me and serve me."

"They just wanted practice so they could do a good job for the clientele."

"I understand, but I'm glad they'll be distracted by some other victims. They made it impossible for me to get any reading done ... every ten minutes asking me if I'd like some more coffee, if the room temperature was too hot or too cold, what entertainment loops I wanted to watch that night, what my preference was for this evening's dining."

"Sounds like they'll do fine. Has the transport ship departed yet?"

Delkin nodded. "The pilot finished unloading supplies, then headed off. He'll be back in four days."

Elisa nodded. That had been her agreement with Lee Iswander. She was only allowed to take the luxury passenger ship so long as it didn't disrupt the more established schedules. She hoped the return ship would arrive before the clients realized they were stranded in the atmosphere of Qhardin.

(•)

The gas giant rotated slowly, so the day was long, providing many hours of sunlight. Elisa called the visitors together for an expedition out among the cloud banks. They all wore jackets in the blowing wind on the loading dock, where a battered old skybus hung connected to the lower module.

Fourth blinked at it in surprise. "That's a piece of junk!"

Elisa couldn't disagree. "It has character. Old Bessie is repurposed equipment left behind when the previous skyminers fled Qhardin in fear of hydrogue attacks."

Roland Kipps crossed his arms over his chest, ignoring the chill wind, while Candeen and Juvia went over to scrutinize the discolored repairs on the skybus's hull. "It's been patched and painted so many times I can't tell where the original ship ends and the repairs begin," said Candeen, and Juvia laughed.

"It's been ten years since Old Bessie qualified to make orbit," Elisa said. She didn't need to mention all the leaks detected on the skybus, the insufficient structural integrity, and a thousand other things that made Old Bessie questionable. But the repairs were good enough to keep it running. "It'll be fine out on the clouds for our tour. Our engineer has tested it several times."

"Let's get aboard," Kipps said. "This is what we came here for."

"I'll take the risk," said Fourth.

Elisa piloted the old skybus away from the Cloud Nine modules. She skimmed across the rising plumes of chemical vapors, then dove into canyons between the atmospheric levels. It was a bumpy ride, and the rattling sounds and unsettlingly loose bangs gave them pause, but Elisa remained confident.

After strapping herself in, Juvia raised her eyebrows. "This is all part of the show isn't it? To make us nervous and increase the thrill."

Elisa hadn't thought of that, but she responded with a shy smile. "I wouldn't reveal our trade secrets." Old Bessie flew past majestic cumulus mountains and bubbling colorful plumes. "Tomorrow I've planned an expedition to the ruined old skymines. You'll find them interesting."

Aware of Old Bessie's safety limitations, she gave a wide berth to the moon-sized whirlpool of an immense hurricane, a maelstrom of mixed gases like a bottomless pit.

"What about the hydrogues down there?" Fourth asked.

Kipps pressed his fingers against the viewing window until his knuckles turned white.

"We haven't seen any sign of them," Elisa said. "We're safe. Just remain calm."

"Whistling past the graveyard," said Candeen. "Isn't that the old phrase?"

"Confidence," Elisa said. "That's the only term I'm interested in."

CHAPTER SIXTEEN

Daniel

While being groomed as a Prince in the old Hansa, Daniel had seen images of the sentient worldtrees on Theroc and the green priests who provided instant communication across the Spiral Arm. But he had never visited Theroc himself. In fact, he hadn't actually done much as Prince, other than say what he was told to say, always ready to take the throne in case King Peter should misbehave.

When Rlinda Kett flew him to the incredible jungle planet, Daniel was stunned by the beauty, the throbbing sense of burgeoning life. It made him almost regret that he had not become King after all. He could have ruled here on this amazing world ... but then his heart felt heavy. If he had stayed with the Hansa, he would never have met Serene, never had his children, never lived in contentment for nine years.

After landing the *Curiosity* on the polymerized treetop canopy, Rlinda escorted Daniel down through the strata of boughs. He inhaled the resinous smell of the worldtrees, heard the humid buzz of insects, the rustle of fronds.

Lifts dropped them down through the high branches to the main fungus reef city, an enormous pale growth that spread out from the gold-scaled trunk of the largest worldtree. The huge hard fungus was riddled with other holes and passages, bubbles that had been turned into offices, shops and living quarters.

Daniel stared. "Is that their palace?"

"That's where the King and Queen live and rule," Rlinda said.

Daniel swallowed hard. He had lived in the towering and ostentatious Whisper Palace on Earth, filled with gold trimmings, grandiose sculptures, vaulted ceilings, marble pillars to show the majesty of the Terran Hanseatic League. That was all behind him now.

Natives and offworlders bustled about on all levels of the tree city. "It's so crowded," he said.

Rlinda laughed. "I should've taken you to Kett Shipping Headquarters—then you would really have gotten a headache."

"I'm not looking for a headache," he said, "I need to find a solution. We have to rescue my people."

"Don't you worry. I'll get us in with the King and Queen right away, and I'll even speak on your behalf." Rlinda stopped in the corridor, turned him to face her. "Here, let me have a look." She brushed the side of his face, stroked his beard. His hair was clean and combed, cut to an acceptable length, and Rlinda had trimmed his beard. She had even laundered his simple clothes in the *Curiosity*'s sanitizers during the flight, and Daniel himself mended them. "You'll never pass for a Prince anymore, but you're acceptable."

He hoped King Peter would know who he was.

The throne room was a bright chamber open to the fresh forest air with flitting butterflies and birds swooping about. Nearly naked green priests stood around the chamber, hairless men and women with emerald skin, who were able to commune with the trees and send their thoughts across the Spiral Arm. Uniformed CDF military officers joined trade representatives and functionaries waiting to see Peter and Estarra.

Rlinda strolled in as if she were meeting an old friend for coffee. The royal couple sat on thrones at the far side of the chamber, and Daniel hesitated as soon as he entered.

Estarra was a beautiful daughter of Theroc with dark skin with rich deep brown hair, bright intelligent eyes, full lips, and a narrow chin. She wore an ornate headdress of feathers, insect carapaces, and colorful moth wings. King Peter was a strong-jawed, handsome man with blond hair and blue eyes, which Daniel knew were artificially created. He himself had undergone similar physical modifications to look more regal and less like his original self.

The King and Queen were listening to another speaker at the moment. In front of the throne stood a bearlike bearded man in a traditional Roamer jumpsuit. The tall man beside him had close-cropped blond hair and flat Nordic features. Daniel recognized Olaf Reeves from the man's earlier visits to Happiness.

The Roamer man spoke intently, his voice rising. "It is about our heritage, Sire. I can see you've not forgotten your connection to Theroc, and Rendezvous was to us what Theroc is to you and the green priests. Without that place, we would not be who we are—and that is why we must rebuild Rendezvous, not just some other station."

Folding his hands together, Peter leaned forward on the throne. "I understand your passion, Mr. Reeves. We know we can't talk you out of your vision, but the rest of the Roamers have clearly made a different decision. For numerous reasons, Newstation is a more appropriate trading and governmental center. It's nearly completed after years of effort and an enormous investment from clan treasuries. We can't simply pull the plug on that."

Estarra added, "That doesn't mean you can't make Rendezvous operational as another trading center. Look at Ulio Station—that's also thriving."

"But in order to make Rendezvous another trading center, I need a great deal more funding," Olaf said. "The project is enormous, and my family has been working for years. It's time the rest of the Roamers come together and help us finish."

Peter frowned sadly. "The Roamers *have* come together, Mr. Reeves."

Olaf looked angry, then deeply disappointed. "That is what I expected you to say, Sire." He and his companion turned to leave. "Thank you for your time."

When they saw Rlinda and Daniel standing there, Olaf was suddenly taken aback.

Rlinda strode forward into the pause. "King Peter, Queen Estarra, I have an urgent matter and a very important guest—someone from your past." She grinned and gestured. "I present the former Prince Daniel. You haven't seen him since the end of the War."

Peter and Estarra stiffened in surprise, and Daniel pushed back his fear and anxiety. "I don't hold any grudge. Honest. I've been gone a long time, and I've been content. You couldn't have done a better thing for me." Daniel considered all the wicked things he had said to Peter back in the Whisper Palace, the threats he had made, parroted from what Chairman Wenceslas had told him. "I'm sorry I forced you to take such extreme actions."

Estarra's surprise covered a flash of her guilt. Peter gave a clipped smile. "And we're sorry it became necessary." He seemed at a loss for words.

Daniel's heart was beating hard. He had dreaded this confrontation, feared that Peter and Estarra would refuse to help. He pressed ahead, insistent. "I have a family now. I live among the neo-Amish on Happiness, an isolated place—as you know." He raised a hand to stop any defense or contradictions. "It doesn't matter. It turned out well. My wife's name is Serene. I have two sons, Enoch and Malachi, and a beautiful daughter, Ruth."

"I've met them," Rlinda said. "Happiness is a pleasant place with honorable hard-working people."

"They're dying," Daniel interrupted. "Unless we do something." Surprised mutters went around the room. "I never wanted to leave that world, never wanted to come back to politics or the government, but I've got nowhere else to turn. If I didn't go through the transportal, I would have been signing a death warrant for my family and for my people."

Olaf Reeves turned to Bjorn, his expression troubled. "What happened, boy?"

Daniel quickly described the rise of the grieka plants, the cyclical wave of the sporeflower infestation and the toxic storm that would soon saturate the atmosphere. "They blossomed first at higher altitudes, and our settlements in the upper meadows are already dying—a third of the people. And now the entire valley is covered with the grieka plants. They were flowering when I left, and it'll only be a few days before the spore pods swell and burst. Then the air will be unbreathable, and people will start to die."

"Do you need us to evacuate your population?" Peter said. "How many are there? We can send CDF ships and whisk them away in a full military operation."

Daniel quailed. "No, that's not—"

Olaf interjected, "You'd be ripping them away from their homes, Sire. During the first cycle, Jeremiah Huystra could have called for help, but the neo-Amish simply endured and then the survivors tried to rebuild. If you save them by force, you'll be doing them no favors."

"But I need to *save them!*" Daniel said. "Last time they tried to survive by wrapping rags over their mouths and noses. That's all the technology they have, but it implies to me that we could get through this with adequate filtration systems, breathing masks, simple protective wear. At least it would increase our chances."

"Is that all you need from us? From the Confederation?" Estarra asked.

When Daniel nodded, looking desperate, Olaf crossed his arms over his chest and huffed. "Why didn't you just ask, boy?"

"Because we have no money to pay for the equipment and materials. I need to beg this as a favor, to throw myself upon your mercy. Please help my people, King Peter and Queen Estarra. We've intentionally not joined the Confederation. We want to be left alone. But now we need help." He swallowed hard. "There's not much time."

The voices in the room built to an uproar, and Peter raised his hands for silence. "Of course we will assist you, Daniel. If you won't let us evacuate your people until the spore storms are over, then we'll give you the filters, masks, airtight seals you need."

"And treatment drugs." Estarra frowned, deep in thought. "Even though we don't have any research about these spores, if it's a severe allergic reaction we must have some generalized potent antihistamines or allergy-dampening treatments. We can help you without destroying your way of life."

"Then I need you to do it," Daniel said, "as soon as possible."

"Roamers have that sort of technology," Olaf said. "Readily available."

"We have some equipment right here on Theroc," Peter said. "The pollen blooms become untenable in certain areas of the worldforest, and we're forced to use protective masks. We can gather a rescue team and load ships right away. We can save your Happiness."

Daniel's lips were trembling, and his throat was thick. He feared that by sending Confederation ships full of well-intentioned rescuers, he would open the floodgates, just as Jeremiah had feared. "I'm worried about bringing so many strangers to our world. How will we keep a low profile then?"

"I've been there myself," Olaf said. "Let me be the one to take him back and deliver the equipment. Roamers know how to use it."

Peter nodded. "Yes, I'd rather have you take Prince Daniel home and help rescue those people without further interference from the Confederation." He turned to Rlinda. "Meanwhile, I've got another mission for my Trade Minister. Rlinda, we need you to make a trip to the Ildiran Empire."

With large, dark eyes, Queen Estarra faced Daniel. "I apologize for what we did to you years ago. If you go back to your planet and decide never to come back, then a lot of things will remain unspoken."

"If you help my people now, there's no conceivable reason why I would still be upset with you," Daniel said. "Just accept my gratitude." Now tears were coming out of his eyes. "Thank you. Thank you so much."

CHAPTER SEVENTEEN

Elisa Enturi

Trying to show off their attentiveness to the Cloud Nine guests, Anil and Shar prepared a fine dinner of preserved and highly seasoned seafood from a water world called Araka. The meal was fancy, but Elisa didn't care for the taste; she had grown up on simpler fare.

The two women from Ulio Station ate a second portion each with great gusto. "We normally have packaged food," said Candeen. "This is a treat."

Fourth complained and compared it to far superior meals he had eaten at expensive resorts. Roland Kipps ate without comment, as if he were simply consuming fuel. His facial scars moved up and down as he chewed.

"We'll take all your comments under advisement in an effort to improve Cloud Nine for expanded operations," Elisa said. "First, we have to prove the system is viable."

"I hope we at least catch a glimpse of hydrogues," said Fourth.

Juvia snorted. "You sound as if you want that."

"I'd love to see them, from a distance. It would break up the boredom."

Elisa continued to find the young man annoying. Kipps said with a growl in his voice, "You don't know what you're talking about."

Candeen said, "People get bored when they don't have the imagination to think of something more useful to do."

Elisa still believed that sky hotels like Cloud Nine would be a lucrative investment for Lee Iswander, but it was becoming more and more apparent that her personality was not suited to being a hostess. She'd chosen these initial guests based on their demographics, not because she thought she might like them, personally. Her focus was on building the business and running operations efficiently. She would never be a socialite. If the sky hotel proved lucrative, sociable receptionists could always be hired.

Frowning, Fourth brushed his long, neatly coifed hair back behind his ear. "When are we going to see something interesting, Ms. Enturi? You promised us a tour of the old skymine wrecks. Yesterday, we only saw a bunch of clouds."

"Qhardin is a gas giant. You shouldn't expect to see much more than clouds," Elisa said, then had to force a smile. "But yes, it's on the schedule. We'll fly out to the wrecked cloud harvester. Engineer Delkin has certified Old Bessie as flightworthy again after our expedition yesterday. We can be on our way."

"Flightworthy?" Fourth snorted. "He must have a flexible definition."

"He has an adequate definition," she said with an edge in her voice. "If you feel uncomfortable, however, you are welcome to remain here by yourself."

"No, I want to see!"

When everyone was aboard the sky bus, Elisa piloted it away from the hotel modules. Because of Qhardin's slow rotation, they still had ten more hours of broad daylight, even though they had already been here for a full standard day. The sunlight dragged on, but once the modular hotel rotated over to the night side, the darkness would last throughout the end of their stay.

Old Bessie rattled under acceleration as Elisa skimmed the clouds, dipping down into bursts of mist. The broad, breathtaking expanse was lovely and impressive, and the horizon seemed more infinite than on any other world she had visited.

Kipps continued to stare into the clouds, as if both dreading and hoping to see a spiked crystalline warglobe. Candeen and Juvia discussed possible recreational activities, even concocting a new sport on the spot, a kind of polo played with skimmerbikes and levitating balls out among the clouds.

They arrived at the huge drifting wreck of the abandoned Roamer cloud harvester. The hemispherical structure rose out of curls of pale yellow mists, and the top of the dome was a forest of antennas and superstructures, exhaust shafts, and evacuation ducts.

"That thing's huge," Juvia said.

"Damned ambitious," Candeen added.

"Cloud harvesters were cities in the skies," Elisa said. "They would drift along at high velocity so the intakes could process enormous amounts of atmospheric hydrogen to produce a tiny amount of ekti."

She circled Bessie around the drifting structure. Some of the great antennas had collapsed, and a few of the hull plates had fallen away. Fourth asked, "Do you think the hydrogues caused all that damage?"

"There's no residue of explosions, no carbonization." Kipps said. "It's just corrosion."

The young man sounded disappointed.

"Probably storm damage," Elisa said. "It's been drifting along for eleven years with no maintenance, slammed by any weather patterns. Notice the axial tilt? One of the levitation engines has failed."

"Maybe you should build your next hotel there," Candeen teased. "Or we could just drag it back to Ulio Station as salvage. We'd fix it up and sell it to some brave Roamer clan."

"You probably could," Elisa said. "*If* the drogues are gone for good."

"Yes," Juvia admitted. "If the drogues are gone. Isn't that what we're all counting on?"

"Can we go aboard and explore?" Fourth asked.

Cruising slowly around the wreck, Elisa could feel the turbulence in the air. The rickety support towers rattled visibly. "Not in these extreme winds, and I wouldn't trust the decks or the levitation engines to be. I can't guarantee your safety." There was nothing Elisa would have liked more than for the arrogant young man to slip and fall out into the cloud decks. "You'll just have to come back for another visit once we've recertified the structure."

"If this skymine is still intact, then the hydrogues must be quiet," said Kipps. "When they hit, they hit mercilessly. On Ubor Major, four warglobes simply appeared over the colony settlement. Our people panicked, some ran to emergency shelters, which had never been designed to withstand hydrogue weapons." He spoke in a trembling voice with his eyes closed, lost in a distant memory." Our colony leader transmitted urgent pleas, he surrendered, he asked the drogues what they wanted." He drew another breath. "What they wanted was just to destroy us. They wanted us all to die." He closed his eyes and retreated into nightmares.

"But you survived," said Fourth. "And think of all the stories you can tell!"

Kipps opened his eyes, flashed him a murderous glare.

Elisa remembered the War, but she had never encountered the hydrogues. For her, the most terrifying time came after the faeros destroyed the Moon and rained cosmic rubble down on the helpless population. Elisa had been trapped on Earth, since her family could not afford to escape. With one gigantic meteor impact after another, she had felt so helpless, unable to do anything but watch the skies and hope. Most of all, she had been angry with her family for being unable to take care of themselves when they needed it....

She drew her thoughts back to the present. "You all accepted the risks when you came here. The hydrogues have been hiding since the end of the War, but they could reappear at any time. Consider this an emergency drill. Watch."

Elisa called up the images that she had brought specifically for this purpose. Originally, she thought it would be chilling, like telling ghost stories around a campfire. "These images were retrieved from the wreckage of another skymine. If the hydrogues had decided to attack, this is what could have happened to the skymine there."

She activated Old Bessie's wallscreens, while the abandoned cloud harvester drifted nearby, rattling in the rising storm winds. On the screens, she projected shaky recordings from another destroyed Roamer skymine. She couldn't remember where the images had been recorded, since she paid little attention to the Roamer clans.

Watching the horrific destruction, she couldn't help but feel awe by the sheer power the hydrogues exhibited. The skymine's cameras captured a swirling disturbance in the clouds, then menacing spiked spheres appeared like bubbles rising from the depths.

Three translucent warglobes rolled up out of the mists, overwhelming the defenseless cloud harvester. The images shook and rattled, as if trembling in fear. Blue lightning crackled from the pointed protrusions as the warglobes charged their weapons.

Projected on Old Bessie's wallscreens, the images were visceral, gut-wrenching. Elisa had reviewed them repeatedly before planning this little exercise. Those who wanted a dangerous and thrilling vacation in Cloud Nine would have all they could want.

Blue lightning danced from the pyramidal protrusions, collecting into a jagged arc that slammed into the skymine. With only a single blast, the drifting Roamer structure was already mortally wounded. The trio of angry warglobes attacked again and again. Explosions tore apart hull plates, structural girders, flaming gas tanks. Finally the screens were filled with static.

Elisa didn't know who had retrieved this recording, or how. As far as she knew, it had never been seen in public before. With the powerful reminder of hydrogue strength, she suddenly had doubts about her confidence that the enemy would not return.

There was a long moment of silence among the passengers. Roland Kipps did not speak, but tears streamed down his cheeks. Old Bessie's projection walls had gone back to their neutral gray, and through the windows, they could see the abandoned skymine drifting in the clouds of Qhardin.

After a long, tense moment, Candeen said with forced humor, "If you'll accept a little advice, Ms. Enturi, maybe you need to fine tune your sales pitch."

CHAPTER EIGHTEEN

Daniel

After Peter and Estarra agreed to help, Daniel was amazed at how swiftly the Confederation came up with possible solutions, not to mention the actual equipment: protective clothing, respirators, filtration masks, and airtight systems that could protect against the toxic grieka spores.

Rlinda Kett had already flown off on her mission to Ildira, and Daniel was anxious to rush off to his family. He felt guilty being on a comfortable planet with amenities, fine foods, and a beautiful climate. He could only think about Serene and their children lying sick during the deadly spore storm. He remembered Jeremiah Huystra, his swollen eyes, his convulsions, and his fever. By now, the leader might well be dead.

He had to go. Now.

Unfortunately, Daniel hadn't brought along a sample of the grieka plant, so the researchers and engineers were operating blind. Within hours, Olaf Reeves and Bjorn Elkand scrounged possibilities from the resources on Theroc and from ships in orbit.

While all the materials and potential drugs were gathered, King Peter invited him to wait. "We're doing everything we can, and as fast as we can."

Estarra added, "In the meantime, we can teach you about what's happened in the Confederation. You have a decade of history to catch up on."

Daniel still felt awkward around the King and Queen. They had much to address, many wounds to heal, explanations to make, but he didn't want to address that, didn't want to be here any longer than necessary.

"I don't need to catch up on it," Daniel said. "I'm going back home. I don't want anything to do with the Confederation."

"Then tell us about your family," Estarra said in a compassionate voice. "We have two children of our own—a son and a daughter, Reynald and Arita."

Daniel's voice trembled when he let himself talk about Serene, Malachi, Enoch, and Ruth. He grew wistful, picturing them in his mind.

In a lull, Peter said in a low voice. "Sorry about what we did to you."

Daniel shrugged. "I deserved it and it was the best thing that ever happened to me. Really, it was."

Before he could explain further, though, Olaf and Bjorn entered the private chamber in the fungus-reef, wearing serious looks. "Our ship is loaded and ready to go, Daniel. We have filtration masks and respirators, anti-allergen treatments, and other basic preventive options. When would you like to go?"

Daniel sprang to his feet. "Right now. I don't want to wait another hour." What if he arrived an hour too late to save Serene? What if the slightest delay of changing clothes or eating a farewell meal cost the lives of his friends?

Peter said, "I can follow up with a CDF crew, under strict secrecy."

Daniel shook his head. "Even if we saved all my people, they would probably shun me if I did that."

Olaf said, "The boy means it, Sire. Bjorn and I will fix the problem as best we can. Let's hope it's enough."

"It'll be enough," Daniel said. "Let's go."

He gave a quick bow, not with the formality and respect Chairman Wenceslas had taught him, but it was enough. Olaf and Bjorn hurried him to the treetop-canopy landing field. Since the Roamer's request for aid to the Rendezvous project had been denied, Olaf seemed just as eager to go.

(•)

Even at top speed, the trip to Happiness would take two days. Daniel tried to figure out how long he'd been gone—no simple task, having moved from planet to planet—and also to calculate the life cycle of the sporeflowers. How long would it take for them to mature and become deadly? By now, many of them must have burst, filling the air with a fog of toxic allergens. Covering their faces with scarves and rags would not be enough to protect the neo-Amish.

He was miserable during the flight, anxious, dreading.

Bjorn was the more conversational of the two. He offered to play games to kill time, teaching Daniel some games of chance, but Daniel kept focusing on his own worries.

More serious, Olaf concentrated on what they would do when they arrived at their destination. The Roamer clan leader pulled up data projections. "Look here, young man. These are different biological protective devices, filters that can block the even tiniest viruses, but you won't need that. Relatively speaking, spores are huge. These simple masks will stop most of the contamination."

Bjorn added, "There must be a critical exposure level. Even filtering ninety percent of the spores will probably reduce the exposures to nonfatal levels."

"But we don't know," Daniel said.

"No, we don't know. Drugs may be more effective. We have a wide variety of broad-spectrum anti-allergens. It'll take some experimentation, and it may not save people who have already inhaled a fatal amount of the toxin, but something's got to work." Olaf called up a final set of images. "As a last resort, we'll use targeted incinerators. We'll destroy any of the grieka plants that haven't yet burst, and do what we can to minimize the next outbreak."

Imagining their fields, the hillsides, the valley, the upper meadows all in flames, Daniel shuddered. "Those spores cover the continent, and they'll keep spreading, carried on the wind. Next cycle they'll all come back."

"And you'll be ready for them," Olaf said. "But only if we find something that works this time."

Bjorn added with a cocky grin on his long face. "I still want to use the targeted incinerators and show those plants we mean business."

"This is a job designed for Roamers," Olaf said. "We're good at surviving in difficult environments, and we know what it means to stay hidden."

Bjorn finished setting up a solitaire game on his own pad. "Think of how many people would die if you didn't try. Life is hard enough, no need to make it harder than necessary. Take help when it's offered."

"We'll accept the help," Daniel said, "so long as the price isn't too high."

"I understand the consequences," Olaf said. "I will keep the price for you and your people at an acceptable level."

They would arrive at Happiness in six hours.

CHAPTER NINETEEN

Rlinda Kett

The seven suns in the Ildiran sky made the entire world dazzle. Rlinda wore protective eye covering, but she still had to squint as she looked at the crystal structures of the capital city sparkling under the glare. It was marvelous.

She had landed the *Curiosity* on an upper diplomatic deck of the Prism Palace. The reconstruction of the exotic palace was more than half completed after the faeros had caused tremendous damage at the end of the Elemental War. The Ildirans had accomplished far more than any human work crews would have done in the same amount of time.

The members of the humanoid alien race were all connected by a faint racial telepathy called *thism*, centered around the Mage-Imperator Jora'h, who had pulled them together to work like a cooperative hive mind on the tremendous task of rebuilding not just the Prism Palace but their entire city.

As Rlinda emerged from the ship, Ildiran noble kith came to meet her with great formality. The nobles were handsome with olive-colored skin and elaborate robes made of reflective strips and shimmering silky fabrics.

She shaded her eyes with a hand and looked around her to see the great city springing up like wildflowers in the desert after a rain. "You will have this place rebuilt in another year or so. It would take the human race fifty years or more to do what you've done here in nine."

"We are impatient to restore the Empire." The Ildiran noble gestured. "Follow me into the Skysphere. The Mage-Imperator will be pleased to see you, as always."

Rlinda had been here many times as Trade Minister. King Peter and Queen Estarra already had a good relationship with Mage-Imperator Jora'h, who was perfectly amenable to negotiating continued commerce with the new Confederation. Not only had Jora'h been an ally of the human race against the deadly elementals, but his soul mate Nira was a human green priest.

The gift that Rlinda had been sent to deliver would be of special interest to Nira.

(•)

Inside the Prism Palace, the Mage-Imperator held court in a cavernous chamber. He sat in his chrysalis chair to receive supplications, but most of his people simply came to gaze upon their godlike leader. The Mage-Imperator was supposed to recline and never let his feet touch the ground, but Jora'h had dispensed with that tradition, impatient with the constraints during the Elemental War.

He was a strikingly handsome man with a strong face and firm jaw, high cheekbones, and a wreath of finely braided hair that wafted around his head like a restless corona. Jora'h stood to greet Rlinda, along with the beautiful female green priest at his side. Nira's emerald skin was smooth, hairless. According to Theron tradition, the green priest wore nothing but a loincloth. Nira's smile widened with delight as she saw what the worker kithmen carried, following Rlinda into the Skysphere audience chamber.

"I come bearing gifts, Mage-Imperator. You'll forgive me if they're intended for the lovely green priest rather than yourself."

He touched Nira's arm. "Any gift for Nira pleases me—especially these."

The four Ildiran workers carried clay pots, each of which held a delicate treeling, an offshoot of the Theron worldtrees. Each one was no more than a foot tall with feathery green fronds and finely scaled gold bark.

"I still have my personal treeling. That's how I remain in contact with the other green priests." Nira caught her breath. "But all of these—ahh, these will be wonderful! Jora'h, we will put them in the rooftop greenhouse dome. There are other Ildiran trees and shrubs there, but the more worldtrees we have, the more we will tie the Ildiran Empire with the Confederation." Her eyes shone.

"We are already very closely bound," Jora'h said, "but for you, I would do anything."

Nira took one of the potted treelings and sat down on the dais steps, placing it on her lap. With delicate fingers she touched the fronds and closed her eyes. Rlinda knew she was using telink, mentally connecting with the interconnected mind of the worldforest. She let out a contented sigh. "The green priests welcome me again. Thank you, Rlinda Kett."

Getting down to business, Rlinda delivered her summary of the new Roamer skymining efforts, asked for trade agreements for increased delivery of the stardrive fuel. "Many Confederation traders also wish to expand ties with the Ildiran Empire. I would have offered our construction teams to help with rebuilding the city, but you seem to have that well in hand."

Jora'h nodded. "The Prism Palace should be restored very soon, exactly the way it was."

Nira's expression darkened. "Nothing will be exactly the way it was. We've all been through too much, and we have too many scars."

"Wounds can heal, and scars can be tough," Rlinda said. "And after the Elemental War, we've all certainly learned how to be tough."

Causing a flurry among the courtiers, a military commander marched into the audience chamber and presented himself before the Mage-Imperator's dais. He wore a scaled officer's robe that extended down to his mid-thighs. His hair had been tied in a braid at the back of his shaved head. Rank symbols and military awards glittered on his chest.

The Mage-Imperator brightened. "Adar Zan'nh, I was just about to tell the Trade Minister our new plans for expanding the Empire."

Rlinda was surprised. Expanding? The Ildirans were known for their lack of innovation, for maintaining their Empire for millennia without change.

Adar Zan'nh blinked. "If that is what you wish to tell her, Liege."

Jora'h motioned, and two attenders came forward with crystalline image projectors, which projected a wire-frame image of a spaceship; a large sweeping model with ornate fins and an elongated body. It looked different from their ubiquitous Solar Navy warliners.

"This is the *Kolpraxa*. After the attacks from the hydrogues and the faeros, we learned and adapted," Jora'h said. "Humans have shown us their imagination, their dreams, and we can learn from this as well."

Rlinda admired the new vessel. "Looks interesting—and huge. What is it designed for?"

"It is an exploration ship. We intend to go beyond the Spiral Arm and see places that no Ildiran has ever seen." Jora'h's voice grew thick with emotion. "I realized after the War that we must know what is out there. The construction of the *Kolpraxa* is in its earliest planning stages, but we will explore."

Rlinda marveled at the sheer audacity of the Ildirans being dreamers and innovators. "Things have changed indeed since the War."

Adar Zan'nh seemed disturbed, and he clearly didn't want to discuss exploration missions. With only a brief glance at Rlinda, he stepped up to the dais, placed his fist in the center of his chest in a sign of respect, then bowed. "There is another matter of some concern, Liege."

"I know." Jora'h dropped his voice. "I felt it in the *thism* as clearly as you did."

Nira reacted with alarm. "What is it, Jora'h? You didn't tell me."

"We lost one of our Solar Navy warliners," said Zan'nh. "A single ship on patrol near the Dhula system, commanded by Qul Loar'nh. Something happened to it."

Jora'h said, "Through the *thism* we felt the alarm of the entire crew. They were injured, dying, but we don't know what happened."

"That's because you don't have green priests aboard your Solar Navy ships," Nira said. "Then you could have instantaneous communication."

"We sensed the emergency immediately," Zan'nh said. "But we have no details. We know only that the ship disappeared. The system has no habitable planets, only two cold gas giants."

"Could it have been hydrogues?" Rlinda asked. "Did they come out and strike?"

"There was no other activity in that sector," said Zan'nh. "We don't even have any splinter colonies there. If the warliner suffered some sort of disaster, no doubt Qul Loar'nh sent transmissions." He bowed before the Mage-Imperator. "I request permission to mount an immediate expedition to investigate."

"Of course, Adar. Gather a septa of warliners and depart when preparations are complete."

Thinking of how she had recently gone to reestablish contact with the lost Hansa colonies, Rlinda said, "I'm good at finding things, and I can depart right now. I'll go have a look."

Adar Zan'nh frowned at her. "With gratitude, Trade Minister, but how could you rescue a Solar Navy warliner?"

"Why do people always underestimate me? We don't even know what happened to the ship."

"It is not your place," Zan'nh said.

Rlinda shrugged. "Just trying to help."

"You have helped a great deal already," Jora'h said. "The treelings you brought will change Nira's life, and for that you have our gratitude. That is enough for today."

Rlinda nodded. "Then I'll be satisfied with that."

CHAPTER TWENTY

Elisa Enturi

In the clouds of Qhardin, Candeen and Juvia goofed around with a pair of small open-frame airbikes that Elisa had sent along to Cloud Nine as a possible recreational activity. It was cold in the open air, so the two women bundled up, strapped in, and zipped out among the misty banks, whooping and shouting.

Grumbling, Oni Delkin tinkered with a third bike as Fourth pranced about, impatient to fly around the clouds as well. The young man stared longingly after them. "You should have had the bikes repaired and ready to go as soon as your guests arrived!"

Delkin fiddled with the engine, pushed the activator and listened to it thrum. "Yes, we should have, but I'm the only one here, and I was busy building the damned hotel for your arrival."

"You should have more engineers then." Fourth groaned as Candeen and Juvia did loops, then plunged down, vanishing into a murky bank.

Elisa stood next to him, arms crossed over her chest. "We'll take that under advisement. I'm just as anxious to get you out there as you are." She saw the clouds growing a ruddy orange as Qhardin's sun finally set.

Finally, with the engine purring, Fourth secured his insulated jacket and climbed on the airbike. He strapped himself in too perfunctorily for Elisa's tastes, and she held him back, personally making sure he was secure. Although the young man annoyed her, she knew any kind of accident or disaster would embarrass Lee Iswander. He had given her carte blanche. He trusted her, and she had proceeded without his detailed knowledge. He wouldn't give it any further thought until she delivered her summary report and proposal—if everything worked well. Losing the son of a very rich and influential family in a stupid accident would not look good in her prospectus.

Fourth roared off the deck, chasing after where the two women had vanished deep into the cloud layers. While he steadied himself on the unfamiliar bike, Candeen and Juvia rocketed up from below, trailing a rooster tail of mist with them as they soared together, laughing. Fourth streaked after them. Roland Kipps had declined to participate in the fun. The grim and shaken war survivor was not here for entertainment.

A signal came in over the comm as a new ship entered the atmosphere, tracking down the cluster of modules. "Calling Cloud Nine, this is Tel Robek, messenger for Iswander Industries. I'm trying to track down Elisa Enturi. Please tell me I have the right system."

Oni Delkin seemed in no hurry to respond, and Elisa reached the comm before he did. "This is Elisa. You're here on Mr. Iswander's behalf?"

"Yes, he sent me. I've been searching, and you're damned hard to find."

"This is a confidential test operation," she answered. "I didn't want to broadcast what we're doing. Is something wrong?"

"He gave me a recorded message. You can hear it for yourself as soon as I land."

The compact scout ship was sleek and new with fine-tuned engines and few amenities, designed to accommodate a single courier or scout. New, fast, and cutting-edge technology—another sign of how Lee Iswander was different. Roamers would have patched up any old wreck and kept it functioning as long as possible without any consideration for appearances.

Robek climbed out, wearing a jumpsuit and a bright red cap, though why he needed a cap when sealed inside a piloting deck, she didn't know. The cap didn't serve him well either, because within five seconds of when he emerged, a strong breeze snatched it away and blew the cap far out into the sky.

Robek yelped. "That was my best cap!"

Elisa didn't care about the cap. "You brought a message for me. I want to hear what Mr. Iswander found so important."

Robek continued to gaze out at the clouds, where his bright cap dwindled to a dot as it drifted away, bouncing on the stray winds.

Then, with a loud cry of delight, the humming airbikes whipped in, Fourth in the lead. He leaned over his bike and raced faster as Juvia and Candeen barreled after him, diving into the cloud bank in search of the lost cap. Robek grinned, waiting.

Elisa cleared her throat. "The message, please."

Distracted, Robek returned with a sealed message crystal. "I don't know what it says. He code-locked it to your voice."

"Of course he did," Elisa said, annoyed and assuming that the pilot had tried to listen. "It's probably confidential business information."

Leaving the man to watch and wait for the three daredevils to retrieve his cap, Elisa cycled back into the main module. The two solicitous servers, Anil and Shar, were busy preparing a fine banquet for when sunset finally arrived on the gas giant. Oni Delkin had returned to the mechanic's bay, so she played Iswander's message in the nearest port, turning the volume down and leaning close. His image appeared on the screen.

"Elisa, I haven't heard a report yet on your plan to create a sky hotel. I look forward to letting you impress me, as you usually do." His expression became serious. "However, we've studied the modules you retrieved from Rendezvous, and I'm afraid they all have structural defects. Since clan Reeves couldn't pay much, we offered older surplus modules, and now we've discovered that their integrity has a tendency to fail, especially under atmospheric conditions."

In the recording, his fingers danced in front of him on a keypad as he uploaded data sets and testing files.

"The four modules I gave you for your sky hotel prototype are from the same model and lot number. I wanted to contact you before you moved forward. I'll get you better modules for your test run, but for the time being, don't use the ones I sent. They're unsafe. They quickly lose integrity, sometimes in as little as a week. We'll scrap them and repurpose the components." He gave her a more personal smile. "Contact me as soon as you get back. I'd like to hear more about your plans." He smiled again, then the transmission ended.

Elisa felt sick and cold. She had wanted to surprise him. She was impatient and ambitious, but also determined to cobble together Cloud Nine. On the other hand, she knew what a publicity debacle any disaster would be. If she made mistakes, Lee Iswander would pay. His reputation, his track record, and his business acumen were on the line. Nobody knew Elisa Enturi, and they would blame Iswander. Her four initial guests were influential, important in their own ways, and they could generate a great deal of bad press if something did indeed go wrong. She hadn't actually cut corners, but she had been anxious to prove her idea, moving forward with all possible speed.

And the luxury transport would not come to pick up the guests for two more days.

She swallowed in a dry throat and went back out to the deck where Tel Robek was waving as the three airbike riders came back up, triumphant. Juvia held the red cap in her hand, but the speed of her flight and the fierce winds blew it out of her grip again, which sent Fourth and Candeen racing after it.

Robek turned to Elisa, grinning. "I think they're going to retrieve it!"

"I assume they will, and they're having fun. Look how much they enjoy being here." She gave a false smile, glad that they were all distracted. "Mr. Robek, I'll need you to stay here for a day or two. I have something important that may need to go back to Mr. Iswander."

The scout pilot shrugged. "If you say so. I'm on salary, and this seems like a nice place."

Leaving him to watch the antics of the race through the clouds, Elisa went to the mechanic's bay and found Oni Delkin lounging about, having completed his work on the bikes. "Mr. Delkin, I want you to check the integrity of these modules. Run complete tests on all systems, all seals, all life-support units."

He frowned at her. "Why? They're self-sufficient."

"Consider it busy work," she said. He would be very busy if seals started failing.

The engineer grudgingly got up and went to retrieve his diagnostics kit.

She hoped he didn't find anything, or if he did, she hoped he found it soon enough. Elisa would not allow any errors on her part to cause embarrassment for Mr. Iswander ... or the deaths of everyone aboard Cloud Nine.

CHAPTER TWENTY-ONE

Garrison Reeves

anting nothing more to do with clan Reeves, Garrison returned to Newstation, a place his father resented on general principles. The orbiting commerce center was now the heart of the Roamer government and economy, the place they had chosen as their thriving heart. The clans had jilted Rendezvous.

Garrison wanted to see if he belonged there.

He flew the *Workhorse* toward the remarkable space station near the glowing comet. The space construction traffic was dizzying, and his navigational screen plotted a safe course among hundreds of ships in the vicinity. The frenetic activity only served to hammer home the difference between Newstation and the broken Rendezvous complex. Even on a busy day, Rendezvous still seemed like a lonely and pitiable ghost town.

After docking, Garrison boarded Newstation, which was awash with Roamer culture, many different colors and accents, the smells of traditional cooking, exotic spices, cuisines developed by necessity and limited ingredients in order to make packaged proteins and carbohydrates palatable.

Trading ships came from countless clan enclaves, outposts on rugged planetoids or inhospitable environments, as well as larger-scale operations on calmer worlds. Garrison's father scorned an easier life, amenities, conveniences, and soft environments. "A knife loses its edge unless it is sharpened." But as he looked around Newstation, he thought the Roamers looked very sharp indeed.

He recognized many people here, having made numerous trips to make fruitless appeals for support. One aloof young man welcomed him, and Garrison recognized Sam Ricks, the second son of a popular Roamer clan, who seemed to make it his mission to know everyone aboard Newstation. Ricks let out a gently teasing laugh. "Are you here to convince us to disassemble Newstation and bring the components to Rendezvous? You should tell your father that race is lost."

Garrison responded with a surprising smile. "I've told him that many times, but he doesn't need facts if he already thinks he knows the answer."

Chuckling, Ricks clapped him on the back. "Your words, not mine! We could use your clan's help here on Newstation. See how we're thriving? This is clearly the wave of the future."

"My father is more interested in the past than in the future."

His attention darting away, Ricks saw someone else he recognized, and he muttered something perfunctory to Garrison, then flitted off without any interest in continuing the conversation.

In his previous visits, Garrison had wanted to solve the problems of clan Reeves, to get investors and workers, to reignite the dream of Rendezvous. Now, when he saw the way other Roamers looked at him, he felt ashamed, realizing what they must have thought of him. He felt his cheeks burn.

He was no longer part of that. After leaving Rendezvous, he did not intend to go back. He was sure that his father felt his grand dreams sliding away, and so he took it out on others ... and the more followers he lost, the tighter a stranglehold he kept on the remaining ones.

Garrison had no regrets about leaving. He had many useful skills; his upbringing had seen to that at least, because a Roamer was supposed to adapt and survive under any circumstances. Now he would survive as an exile from his clan, but not from the rest of the Roamers.

For a moment he thought of Sendra Detemer, the strong and beautiful young woman who would likely have been his wife if he'd remained at Rendezvous. She was the obvious choice, and even Olaf approved. If she did marry him, maybe the two of them would be strong enough to stand up to his father ... but did he actually want to be the next clan leader? Was he willing to have that kind of fight? No, he didn't think so. Garrison was not power hungry, did not need wealth or influence, did not want to reshape Roamer history. The clans were making their own history here at Newstation. He had no intention of interfering with that.

But he was still a Roamer in his heart, and he thought about what his people really stood for. The clans were problem solvers—but Olaf Reeves wasn't trying to solve a problem. He was creating a problem by burying himself in the past. Garrison grumbled to himself. When had Roamers ever been stuck in the past? Wasn't it better to construct something new and exciting than to rebuild something old and broken?

He spent time on Newstation, drinking in the conversation, the restaurants, the entertainment centers, the coffee and klee houses where clan members discussed business or gossip. Veterans of the Elemental War told grim stories, while others talked about grand dreams and giant projects. Kotto Okiah, the greatest Roamer scientist, had launched a breathtaking new scientific project in the Fireheart Nebula. Kotto's "Big Ring" would take years to complete and cost an inconceivable amount of money, but the Roamers supported it because they liked to dream big. They looked to the future, expanded beyond what they had.

Unlike Olaf Reeves.

By contrast, Garrison thought of Iswander Industries back on Earth, and especially Elisa Enturi. She was beautiful and intelligent, with a common sense unlike anything he saw among his family. Elisa had thrown her lot in with Lee Iswander, a new sort of Roamer. Many of the clans disliked Iswander because his attitudes and business practices seemed too much like the corrupt Hansa.

But was that a bad thing? Iswander ran his operations for profit and efficiency, and also to help fill obvious needs. Garrison had heard other people mutter that the man wasn't a real Roamer, but now that he knew more about Iswander's practices and what he intended to accomplish, Garrison felt a spark of anger rise within him.

Who was more of a "real Roamer?" An inflexible old fossil like Olaf, or a person who solved problems and seized opportunities? Someone like Lee Iswander. Someone like Elisa Enturi.

Garrison spent another day at Newstation, talking to people, seeing the sights and gathering information. But he had already made up his mind.

He departed in the *Workhorse*, flying back to Earth. Flying back to find Elisa.

CHAPTER TWENTY-TWO

Rlinda Kett

After delivering her potted treelings to Ildira, Rlinda was anxious to depart for her own reasons. While Adar Zan'nh put together a cumbersome expeditionary force to investigate the missing Solar Navy warliner, she bid her farewells to the Mage-Imperator and accepted a warm hug from the green priest.

"Thank you for the wonderful gift from Theroc," Nira said. "When those treelings grow tall, they will make me feel more at home."

During her meetings in the Prism Palace, Rlinda had secured several trade agreements and paved the way for Confederation manufacturers to deliver unique items to the Ildiran Empire. She had even negotiated a grant of land, a portion of the capital city where a group of humans could settle among the Ildirans. They would share their traditions and cultures in an exchange of goodwill among races. Countless humans were fascinated by the alien race, and already a dozen ambitious families were eager to set up shop to demonstrate arts and crafts, cook human specialties, and cater to what they hoped would be an equally fascinated Ildiran audience.

Overall, it was a good mission. Peter and Estarra would be pleased.

Rlinda departed as quickly as possible, knowing she could move faster than the tradition-bound Solar Navy. The Ildirans were a people trapped by their ceremonies, and nothing formal could be done without complex, tedious planning. She worried that the lost warliner might be in some kind of continuing danger, although the Adar and the Mage-Imperator seemed certain the crew were already dead, from what they could sense through the *thism*. Rlinda, though, held out hope, and she intended to get there first.

The Ildirans knew the patrol path of the lost warliner, near a star system called Dhula. From Adar Zan'nh's briefing, Rlinda knew Qul Loar'nh's schedule and approximately when some kind of disaster had occurred. That gave her the parameters she needed, and she could interpolate where the ship might be. She went hunting.

The *Voracious Curiosity* flew into the blindingly bright sky, reached orbit, and raced off in the direction of the Dhula system. Rlinda was counting on the fact that Loar'nh would have sent some kind of distress signal, even though he knew the electromagnetic message could not possibly go far enough and fast enough to summon help in time.

But the speed of light was a constant, and knowing the approximate time when such a distress would have been sent, as well as the general location of the warliner, Rlinda could fly into the signal bubble, the radius a signal could have traveled. If she could intercept the distress message, she could learn what had happened to the warliner, and then she could head in to rescue any survivors, or at the very least find an emergency log.

Knowing the Ildirans, Zan'nh would bring his ships into the vicinity and crisscross a vast gulf of space in a rigid search pattern until they blundered upon the warliner. Rlinda could act much faster than that, and she would consider it a favor for the Mage-Imperator. Also, if the warliner was wrecked, the Ildirans would likely abandon it, and in that case Rlinda could claim it as salvage, maybe turn it over to the ambitious repair engineers from Ulio Station.

She relished a challenge.

As the *Curiosity* flew onward, Rlinda rummaged in the left pocket of her slacks and removed the silver capsule, placing it on the flat surface of the piloting controls. "I wish you were here to help me make the plotting and course suggestions, BeBob. You were always better at that than me."

Of course, BeBob would never have gone chasing after a missing Ildiran warship in the first place, especially knowing the entire Solar Navy would be hunting for it too. But Rlinda had been perfectly happy to push her favorite ex-husband out of his comfort zone. Sometimes a person just needed a little shove.

She slowed the ship when she was within four light days from the Dhula system, figuring she was still half a day out from the transmission boundary. She eased forward, her comm system fully active, scanning all bands. She didn't want to go too fast and overshoot the message, but the comm filters would intercept the signal as soon as they encountered it—if Qul Loar'nh had even sent out a message. What if the warliner commander hadn't even bothered, knowing that the Mage-Imperator would pick up on his crew's distress through the *thism*?

No, a commander would have tried every possible hope. There was always a chance some Roamer scout or Confederation trader might be in the area. Or maybe Loar'nh had launched a log buoy, some kind of reporting drone, which would have a locator, a ping signal.

The *Curiosity* rolled forward for an hour, and then she got bored and went back to the galley to fix herself a snack. But a snack was inadequate unless it had accompaniments. Crackers had to be toasted, the cheeses paired with an appropriate chutney. Then she decided that cheese and crackers needed to have a savory soup. Rlinda was never satisfied with packaged soups, so she used tomato basil as a base and added her favorite ingredients, roasted garlic, rosemary, and a sprinkle of crushed walnuts on top.

Then, of course, such a snack had to be enjoyed with the proper wine, and she had a bottle of good New Portugal red. She opened it and poured herself a glass, but in order to enjoy it properly, the wine had to breathe. While the wine breathed, she chose a good selection of music, BeBob's favorite—Relleker jazz.

She hadn't liked the style much herself, but she was feeling nostalgic and she played it for him.

By the time she finished her light snack, two more hours had passed. She went back to her expanded piloting chair and lounged in front of the controls, sipping the last of her second glass of wine, when the comm alert triggered, "Message received."

Rlinda sat up so quickly she almost spilled her wine. She slowed the *Curiosity* and ran the message back through the filter, replaying it. The transmission showed a distraught Ildiran military officer—Qul Loar'nh, she presumed. The commander spoke in a monotonous deadpan as though he had lost all hope, simply delivering a report.

"... simultaneous catastrophic failure of reactor shielding on two stardrives. We lost our ability to fly, and the barrier walls failed before we could put dampeners or radiation shields in place. Most of our ekti spilled into space, but I prevented an explosion." He paused, drew a breath. "We're dead anyway. Life-support systems have been compromised in a cascading surge. There's a slim chance our engineers might get them fixed, but it will not matter. Every person on board has received a lethal radiation dose. The engineer kith down in the stardrive chambers are already dying. The medical kith tested the rest of us and confirmed that tissue damage has set in. The warrior kith are the most susceptible, and they will die next."

He paused, as if concentrating. "According to the tests, I expect to be dead within a day. The last ones to remain alive will be the attenders, but they will have no one to attend. I am making preparations, Liege. They will take care of the bodies and prepare them in hopes that someday they may be brought back to Ildira and burned under the light of the seven suns.

"Through the *thism* you already know something terrible has happened to us. If someone finds our ship, the complete log is in the command nucleus. My crew and I have been proud to serve you, Mage-Imperator Jora'h, and the Ildiran Empire."

He placed a trembling fist in the center of his chest and bowed his head. Then the transmission ended.

Rlinda held the wine in her hand and stared at the screen, contemplating whether or not she wanted to watch the message again. She decided not to. In a single gulp she finished her wine, then traced the origin of the signal, tracking it back to the heart of the Dhula system, near the larger gas giant. The ship must have been on patrol when it suffered its stardrive mishap.

She slid the silver capsule aside so she could get at her navigation controls. "Let's go find it, BeBob."

CHAPTER TWENTY-THREE

Elisa Enturi

As night settled in on Qhardin, the modular sky hotel sank into the clouds where the running lights illuminated the swirling chemical mists with an eerie glow. Meanwhile, Oni Delkin grudgingly but diligently moved around the modules, running standard diagnostics but not knowing why.

Anil and Shar had crafted a fine meal for the guests as well as the visiting scout pilot. Tel Robek dove into the full five-course meal in the common area and even asked for seconds. Elisa told the scout pilot to eat and drink whatever he liked. "Make yourself comfortable, Mr. Robek. I need to check something before we send you back to Mr. Iswander." The pilot didn't mind. He occupied himself with the wine list, checking selections of expensive vintages he had always wanted to try.

After dinner, laughing and exhausted from their flying exercises, Candeen and Juvia went back to their quarters, wrapped up in their own company. Roland Kipps sat in the reading alcove, while Fourth amused himself by playing solitary games in the common room.

Elisa was glad to find them all occupied, because she didn't feel terribly sociable—not that she ever did. She remained tense after Lee Iswander's disturbing message, flinching with every creak or unexpected noise she heard.

She tracked down Delkin in the mechanic's deck, which held the main processors, life-support systems, and levitation engines. When she entered, she caught the man sitting down and relaxing. Her voice was razor sharp. "How is the inspection going?"

Embarrassed, he pulled himself to his feet. "Mostly done. I was just taking a break."

"You can take a break when you finish."

He shot her an annoyed look. "Why are you in such a hurry for this useless busy work? The modules are self-sufficient, and I checked all the systems when we assembled Cloud Nine less than two weeks ago."

"Then it's time for the two-week check. I just received new information from Mr. Iswander. There may be a problem with the integrity of this unit."

With an exaggerated sigh, Delkin picked up his equipment again, then began walking around the mechanic's bay, testing each one of the wall plate junctures and the union where this module connected to two others.

"Safety and double safety—I know. Tolerances are set by paranoid people. Roamers used to put just about anything together and make it work, but Iswander Industries is a stickler. There's nothing to worry about, honest."

He played a scanner over a support rib and a hull seam, rapped on the juncture with his knuckles to produce a satisfying metal sound.

"Just keep checking," she said.

The engineer moved around the chamber, tested the electronic web that ran through the sandwiched hulls, the larger energy conduits, the life-support channels. Cloud Nine drew all its energy from three high-capacity power blocks. "Everything's in peak shape, Elisa, just like I said."

She watched and waited. "That's what I wanted to hear."

Delkin went over to the union of the modules where he ran the scanner around, then frowned as a sequence of green lights turned amber. He double-checked and triple-checked, then watched several readings turn red. "Hmm, that didn't show up before. These two modules aren't constructed properly. The combined seal isn't as strong as it should be."

He traced the structural anchor from the seal, walking slowly around the opposite side of the module, scanning the smooth metal walls. Elisa watched him intently as he muttered. "This module shows a weakness. Something's not put together right. The fusion of these plates, it's ..." He held up the scanner and rapped again with his knuckles. "Some kind of corrosion, a breakdown due to pressurization? Maybe something in the atmosphere of Qhardin?" He pounded harder on the metal, listening to the sound. "It should hold, though." He struck one more time.

A sudden crack zigzagged down the middle of the hull where one sheet had been joined to another. The two plates simply split apart, the crack widening to more than a foot in a fraction of a second.

Delkin gaped, and the module's internal pressure burst the hull plates out before he could utter a sound. The Cloud Nine engineer was sucked out into the open void, whipped into the swirling clouds. A full second later, his distant scream came from far out of sight.

Elisa scrambled to find a stable grip. Air roared through the damaged module, scattering loose debris Delkin had left lying about. If she stumbled, she would plunge into the gas giant's emptiness herself, but she held on, clawing for balance, dragging herself toward the nearest hatch.

The breach destabilized the entire module complex, and the decks began to tilt. She reached the connecting passage and pulled herself through the airlock into the next module. On the opposite wall, the adjoining module connected to the mechanic's deck begin to wrench apart.

It was a cascade of problems, one tipping point, then a succession of disasters. Elisa realized that she had never done an emergency briefing with the guests because she never expected anything to go wrong. Even with the howling alarms, they had no evacuation plan, no muster point, no survival systems. She had intended to add those later. Cloud Nine had no escape pods, no emergency lifeboat. The only ships were Tel Robek's one-man scout craft and Old Bessie the skybus.

Poor planning. Poor management. Countless safety violations. She could already hear the ringing condemnations. Once word got out, her serious lack of judgment would be plain for all to see— but Elisa Enturi wouldn't be the one to pay the price. Oh, she would certainly be sacked, if not convicted of criminal negligence ... if she survived at all. Lee Iswander would take the blame for so many cut corners, so many improbable conclusions, misleading promises ... obliviously placing innocent customers in danger, *important* customers.

Iswander would be excoriated, ruined. He would lose all credibility. He might even end up in jail. And it was her fault.

She sealed the airlock behind her and struggled into the community module. Behind her, roaring sounds came from the mechanic's deck where the broken module continued to tear itself apart. The adjacent habitation module had come loose, its seal pulling apart. The four guests had their quarters there, but right now only Candeen and Juvia were back in their rooms. Roland Kipps and Fourth were in the community module.

Once through the hatch, just as Elisa grabbed an anchored cabinet to secure herself, she watched as the habitation module ripped itself away, breaking its connection to the damaged mechanic's deck. The entire module tumbled away from the core.

Through the observation port, Elisa could see, just for a moment, the two women inside scrambling for safety ... but there was no safety. The module wall was breached, the doorway gaping open. Juvia held on to the fringe, screaming, while Candeen was sucked out into the open gases. Without levitation engines of its own, the module dropped like a stone, vanishing into the depths. Both women were gone.

Elisa gasped, her thoughts spinning. The lights flickered in the community module, but the automated alarms continued to blare. Only two of the four modules remained—but the damaged mechanic's deck held the systems that kept them aloft, and now the Cloud Nine complex was failing. Life support would go next.

They had to get out of here, but there was no way to escape— and she saw no way to cover up her own mistakes.

Roland Kipps looked sick with panic. He staggered forward, clutching for balance, holding on to the tilting wall. Fourth stumbled after him, tripped and sprawled onto the sloping deck. The walls were shaking, but remained intact. For now. Elisa already saw some of the hull plates cracking, though. The complex was falling apart. The components couldn't withstand the added stresses of the cascading disasters.

Fourth scrambled to his hands and knees, then pulled himself to his feet by gripping the wall. His face was pale and slack. "What's happening?" Then his eyes went wider. "Is it a hydrogue attack?"

Kipps looked grim. "It's hydrogues—has to be. They'll blast us apart in the clouds."

Elisa caught her breath as an idea sparked through her mind. "Hydrogues ... yes, yes it is."

CHAPTER TWENTY-FOUR

Rlinda Kett

As the *Curiosity* flew into the Dhula system, homing in on the Ildiran distress call, Rlinda listened to the weakening transmissions from the dying crew. Qul Loar'nh was haggard, his skin tone blotchy, his cheeks sagging. His voice burbled as mucous filled his lungs from the continued radiation damage.

"Two thirds of mm crew are dead, and the attenders are preparing the bodies. Eventually, the Solar Navy will find us, but they will not be in time. Even if they do, there is no way they can help us. The warrior kith succumbed first, but by being a halfbreed noble and warrior, I have more immunity. Our ship is adrift, life support failing. The engineers are all dead."

He drew a deep, rattling breath. "Under other circumstances, I might just have considered driving the reactor into overload and vaporizing all of us to end this pain ... make a clean end." His expression fell. "But our stardrive has failed, the reactors silent. I have no way of doing such a thing. We must linger ... and die one by one. The *thism* among us is frayed. Some of the technicians have gone insane from brain damage caused by the radiation." He shook his head. "That seems worse than this debilitating illness."

Behind him, the command nucleus was dim and empty. Half of the stations were empty. The warliner continued to drift, not far from the uninhabited gas giant. Loar'nh ended the transmission.

Rlinda's comm remained silent for some time as she flew closer, knowing the wrecked warliner was not far ahead. Finally, another transmission wave came in, and on the screen she saw the Ildiran commander's hand barely twitching on the controls. His eyes were closed, his face slack. His head jerked from side to side with nerve and muscle convulsions. Loar'nh simply sagged and slumped, could not say a thing, and then sat motionless for the rest of the transmission. With an ache in her heart, Rlinda switched off the comm and ending that poignant silence. There was nothing more for her to see.

Within the next hour she could see the Dhula gas giant ahead. Even though the warliner's power systems had died down, she still detected a bright thermal image, giving off energy in the infrared, although surely everyone aboard was dead by now. Zan'nh and Jora'h had been right, sensing through the *thism* that the crew had perished, so they had felt no urgency in rushing out to find the damaged ship.

But Rlinda cruised in, intending to investigate, take images, and install a beacon so Adar Zan'nh and his recovery crew could easily locate the ship—just as a favor, being a good neighbor.

When the *Curiosity* closed in on the drifting warliner, she was surprised to see all the frenetic activity in the vicinity. Because she assumed the ship was just a drifting derelict, she approached with her running lights on, not attempting to hide. Her active sensors mapped out the vicinity in front of her, pinger pulses locking the specific position of the ornate alien warship as she decelerated.

Rlinda had seen many Ildiran warliners, with their distinctively anodized hull plates and great extended solar-sail fins. But this warliner was *crawling* with black, angular forms that scuttled about on the exterior surface. The rear stardrive engines glowed a deep, dull red from residual radiation bleeding into space, but the skittering shapes outside the ship were not affected by either the radiation or the vacuum of space.

Seeing the activity, Rlinda wondered if some massive salvage crew had claimed the wreck, but then she saw angular black ships drifting near the warliner's bow: smaller, ominous-looking craft that hovered in place. More black figures emerged, like beetles that landed on the warliner's outer hull and began disassembling the ship.

Black robots.

Rlinda felt cold and astonished. The Klikiss robots had been one of the most terrible enemies during the Elemental War. They had betrayed the human race and nearly destroyed the space military. Originally designed and built by the insect race, the black robots were malicious and destructive, but Rlinda had thought they had all been exterminated.

Obviously not.

Hundreds of black robots swarmed over the warliner, stripping it down for materials, taking away the components ... possibly building something elsewhere. They had already peeled away a quarter of the hull, stacking and delivering the hull plates to the black geometric ships, which flew off while more robots continued to deconstruct the Ildiran vessel.

"This is not a good day," she muttered, just as a squeal of incomprehensible static and a chittering burst of language appeared over her comm speakers. The *Curiosity*'s sensors began to overload as a thousand directed transmissions hammered her shields. Two of the angular black ships began to accelerate toward her.

Rlinda immediately activated her engines and her shields. "No, not a good day at all."

Stirred up like angry hornets, the black robots came after her.

CHAPTER TWENTY-FIVE

Daniel

When the rescue ship arrived, Happiness was infested with the beautiful but deadly spore-flowers. They had blossomed in waves, magenta and white petals unfolding from the fleshy spore pod. The first wave had already shriveled and died, and the swollen pods burst to spew a deadly miasma into the valley.

As the Roamer ship landed outside the village, Daniel pressed his hands against the observation ports. His eyes stung with tears as he searched for activity below. He saw smears of smoke from smaller fires, but most of the homes looked silent, shuttered up, empty ... or dead. "Can't you land any faster?"

Olaf brought the ship down hard, crushing an entire patch of the grieka flowers which had infested a field. He was grim at the controls. "By the Guiding Star, it isn't going to be difficult to collect a sample of spores so I can run tests."

"We need to know as soon as possible." Daniel swallowed hard, pressing his face against the windowport. "One of the drugs we brought *has* to treat the spores. It'll make my people immune."

Then Daniel spotted all the fresh mounds of dirt in the community cemetery. Four bearded men in dark garments and wide-brimmed hats worked shoulder to shoulder with shovels, digging more graves.

As soon as the ship had come to rest, Daniel went to the hatch. "I need to see if my family's all right. I have to check on them. We've got to help!"

Before he could activate the controls, Olaf grabbed him by the collar. "Not yet! You know the air is thick with toxic spores, and you have no resistance."

Daniel spun, his face distraught. "Inject me with one of the broad-spectrum anti-allergens. It better be sufficient."

"No," Olaf said firmly, and went to the supply cabinet. "I have complete decontamination gear for the three of us. We'll suit up and distribute respirators and breathing masks for all the others."

Daniel shook his head. "I won't wear a decontamination suit if my people aren't."

Olaf blew air through his lips, annoyed but understanding. "I didn't think so." He pulled out a full facemask respirator. "This will seal around your face, eyes, mouth, and nose. Use it, at least for now. It should filter out all the spores and you can breathe. If you're sick, you can't help."

Bjorn broke in. "Could be that we three are the only healthy people on this world. If you have an allergic reaction and collapse, you'd leave altogether too much work for Olaf and me."

Daniel's shoulders slumped, but he was anxious to get out there. Olaf handed him the bug-like facemask, the transparent shield. He adjusted the mask, made sure the gaskets sealed to his sweat-dampened skin. When he breathed, the dry air tasted of a faint chemical tang. His voice was muffled. "One look at us and my people will see us as monsters ... maybe as bad as the Klikiss who would have come through the transportal."

Olaf and Bjorn both stepped into their decontamination suits, pulling the fabric up over their torsos and sealing them. "We might look like monsters, but we will be *rescuers*."

Daniel stared at the ship's access hatch. "Hurry. Can't you hurry?" He pressed his hands against the observation windows again and saw several weak, stick-like neo-Amish heading toward the ship. They moved unsteadily, their faces swollen and blotchy. They could barely see through puffy eyes. "Or let me out there myself. I have to see my family."

All those graves ...

In the previous cyclical infestation of sporeflowers, one in three neo-Amish had died. What about his children, his wife?

Olaf and Bjorn finished suiting up. "We're ready now."

Olaf took a medkit with all the anti-allergen medications, while Bjorn fiddled with an analysis pack. "I'll grab some sporeflowers and run tests. We *may* be able to determine the most effective blockers in less than fifteen minutes."

The ship's hatch opened into a swirling yellow fog, thin, but poisonous.

Wearing his traditional, but cleaned, clothes, Daniel strode out, adjusting the respirator across his face. He placed his wide-brimmed hat on his head, knowing how odd and frightening he must look.

He recognized several of the men coming toward them. All had cloths wrapped around their mouths and noses, but their swollen eyes indicated how much their bodies were reacting to the spores. "Daniel, you came back! We thought you'd escaped and left us."

"I wanted to save you. I brought these people from the Confederation," he said. "They have masks and medicines to cure us."

The neo-Amish men looked at one another. One said, "Father Jeremiah told us you had gone back to your real people, that you were never one of us."

"I went to get help," Daniel insisted.

"Jeremiah's dead," said one of the others, as if angry at the man's stubbornness. "We buried him first, and now we've buried twelve more."

"My family?" Daniel asked, and his voice cracked. "Serene? The three children?"

"We don't know. Everyone is shut up in their homes, doors and windows sealed. It's the best we can do. We try to watch out for one another." He sucked a deep breath through the cloth over his mouth. "Not many of us are strong enough to make the rounds anymore."

In his decon suit, Bjorn collected specimens from the ripened sporeflowers. As he plucked one of the pods from a drooping stem, it burst in his hands, spraying spores everywhere. He scraped some into his portable scanner, running the first round of analyses.

Daniel bolted off to his home where the windows were shuttered. He pounded on the door, shouting through the muffling facemask. "Serene, I've come back!" Knowing that none of the homes among the neo-Amish possessed any sort of lock on the door, he shoved against the wood, pushing aside wadded rags his family had stuffed around the cracks.

The interior was dim, but he saw people moving about, Serene and one of his boys ... Enoch. His other two children, Ruth and Malachi, were stretched out on beds, moaning and shivering, their faces a horror of bloated swellings, running mucus. He could barely recognize them.

A bucket of well water sat next to their beds, its surface scummy with drifting spores. So weary she could barely move, Serene drenched a rag in the bucket, then mopped Ruth's face, smearing the thick mucus oozing from the girl's eyes and nose. Ruth moaned and squirmed.

"You're alive!" he cried as he burst inside. "Are they all alive?"

When Serene looked up at him, he reeled. Her face looked as bad as Rickard had when he'd staggered in from the upper meadows. "Malachi's barely breathing," she said, then sighed.

He embraced her, though she had little strength to respond. "Look, I brought help, just as I promised. The Roamers brought medicine, equipment, supplies that should protect us against the spores."

"We've been praying," Serene said. "Some of us will survive. We are all strong."

"You'll be stronger with help," Daniel insisted as he wrestled with his own contradictory feelings. He had been reluctant to bring miracle cures or easy solutions from the Confederation, knowing how these people would resent it. But one look at his dying son changed his mind.

Serene could barely recognize Daniel, with her eyes so swollen that her vision must be blurred and uncertain. When he touched her forehead, it was burning hot. On the bed, Malachi squirmed and coughed; his breathing was just a thin, difficult wheeze burbling through mucus.

Olaf, appeared at the doorway in his full decontamination suit, carrying his medical pack from which he removed a sealed envelope. With gloved hands, he cracked open the envelope and unfolded moist, disinfectant towels. "Use these to wipe their faces. There's an anti-inflammatory. It'll feel soothing, at least until I receive word from Bjorn about the best drug to use."

Daniel mopped Serene's face with one of the cloths, clearing the mucus and perspiration so he could see and remember how beautiful she was. His heart ached, knowing the pain and sickness she had endured from this scourge that Happiness itself had thrown against them. She seemed afraid and resistant, but as he lovingly cleaned her, she relaxed and sighed. "It's a blessing," she said.

Daniel took another of the cloths and bent over Malachi in the cot. The young boy seemed to respond, relaxing as his face was cleaned with something better than the spore-thickened water bucket.

Next, Daniel tended to Ruth and then Enoch, who was helping his mother, though the boy seemed in a daze himself. Olaf touched the side of his head, listening to a comm transmission in his ear. Daniel could hear Bjorn's words from the comm speaker. "Four of our broad-spectrum anti-allergens should let them breathe better and reduce the swelling. I've already administered it to the workers out here, and it's done wonders."

Olaf opened his medical kit, asking Bjorn to identify the specific drug to use. Without asking, he injected Malachi first. Serene moved protectively closer, grumbling. "What is that? What are you doing to him?"

"We're saving him," Olaf said.

Daniel offered the next injection to Serene. She tried to turn him down, but he insisted. "Our children need their mother."

"I'll be fine," she said.

"Yes, you will be," he insisted, and injected her.

When his family members had been treated, Olaf said, "Let them rest. Daniel, we have all the rest of your people to save. We need your help"

When Daniel took a longing look at his family, they seemed better already. The fast-acting anti-allergen was used for emergency rescue, and this was indeed an emergency.

"I will be back shortly," he promised Serene. He made her lie down on their bed. "Don't worry, the children are taken care of. We're all taken care of."

(•)

The two Roamer men stayed to help, as the neo-Amish began to turn the corner after the spore storm.

Seventeen of the suffering people vehemently refused any outside help, and after trying to convince them, Daniel let them have their way. Of those seventeen, six died—exactly as the percentages should have been.

No, not as they *should have been*, Daniel thought, because they should all have been saved with a simple, obvious treatment. Olaf Reeves said he understood their reasons and their resistance, but that did not make Daniel feel better.

He kept shaking his head. "They didn't need to die. It was such a simple thing. Face masks, anti-allergens, filters, seals. All so easy ..." He thought of how many conveniences and wonders of civilization the Confederation had to offer, but he blocked those thoughts. "It's all so tempting," he said.

Nodding, Olaf crossed his arms over his chest. After taking the anti-allergens themselves, he and Bjorn had eschewed the decontamination suits, although they still wore face masks to minimize the exposure.

"There's a fine line between temptation and necessity," Daniel said.

"Not a fine line at all," Olaf replied. "If your beliefs are strong enough, you do what's right. And what is *right* is to save your people. You did that." He snorted. "Dead people can have firmly held beliefs, but do no one any good. Saving them doesn't mean you throw away everything you are." He set his jaw. "As long as you set boundaries and remember your core." He seemed to be thinking of himself rather than the neo-Amish.

Daniel was overjoyed just to know his family had been saved. The village cemetery had more graves now, but would have been expanded far more if Daniel hadn't brought help.

He frowned, though. "Next time it will be easier to ask for assistance ... for good or bad."

He stared across the valley floor at the neo-Amish settlement. Most of the grieka spore flowers were withered now, their pods burst, the spores in the air. Carrying targeted incinerators, he and Olaf, and any neo-Amish volunteers, would cross the valley floor and torch the spores. The flames already crackled high, and Bjorn seemed happy with the useful destruction he was causing.

CHAPTER TWENTY-SIX

Rlinda Kett

As the black robot ships swooped out to intercept her, Rlinda's hands reacted instinctively, working over the *Curiosity*'s controls. "Here we go again." With her big palm, she swept up the capsule of BeBob's ashes and tucked it safely in her pocket, then punched her engines and accelerated upward in a high-G curve.

At the half-dismantled Solar Navy warliner, more robot ships ignited their engines and raced after her. Rlinda knew the black robots could endure far higher accelerations than she could, and she already felt the giant hand of gravitational forces pressing her back against the expanded seat. "This reminds me too damned much of the War."

Rlinda and BeBob had flown many missions together, fleeing hydrogue warglobes or faeros fireballs, dodging black robot attackers and even obnoxious EDF battleships trying to intercept them, but she'd had the last nine years to get rusty doing business as Trade Minister, making milk runs, rebuilding civilization.

But she remembered her stuff quickly enough.

The black ships closed the gap and opened fire before they had achieved a target lock. Even though Rlinda could barely lift her hand against the extreme acceleration, she put the *Curiosity* into a corkscrew, spinning and looping with evasive actions.

She knew she could not outfly the robots. Since they were obviously dismantling the Ildiran warliner for components, no doubt they wanted to neutralize and then salvage the *Curiosity* as well—and Rlinda vowed not to let them have that.

Barely able to breathe through gritted teeth, she moved a heavy hand to the comm controls and broadcast an all-spectrum distress beacon, knowing that it would do her no more good than it had Qul Loar'nh, but at least someone would learn what had happened to her, if she didn't manage to fly out of this.

"I have located a derelict Solar Navy warliner, all crew dead. Coming upon the wreck"—She paused to take a deep breath against the gravitational boulders on top of her chest—"I found it crawling with Klikiss robots who were dismantling the ship for some purpose. You can bet they're not donating all proceeds to charity. Now the damned robots are after me. Trying to remember my dogfighting skills from the War." She tried to think of anything brilliant or memorable to say, since this might well be her last transmission, but she came up empty handed. "If there's any help available in the neighborhood, I'd appreciate it. Don't wait too long."

She dramatically altered course again, looping back and cutting speed. The pursuing robots streaked past her, accelerating too quickly to react in time. As the black ships flashed past, she fired her aft jazers and damaged one of the pursuing craft, more through luck than skill. It spun, tumbling out of control.

Now, all she had to do was worry about the rest of them.

She launched another scattershot of jazer blasts, and one energy beam scored the underbelly of a black ship, breaching the hull plates. But the vessel kept flying, even with the severe damage.

"Damned robots," she muttered.

Her only chance was to dive into the Dhula system, straight for the gas giant. With all those moons and a partial ring of scattered debris, she might be able to play hide and seek. Worst case, she could plunge into the clouds of Dhula itself.

The gas giant lay ahead of her. Rlinda increased speed until she couldn't even breathe, but she endured. If the bugbots caught up to her, she wouldn't be breathing any longer.

The *Curiosity* dove toward the gas giant's equator. Dhula had at least seven major moons, and her scanners showed bounce-back images from several hundred pieces of space debris. In similar systems, she might have expected to find some uncharted Roamer base, asteroid-mining operations, or even cloud harvesters. But Dhula genuinely had nothing of interest from a commercial perspective. No cavalry was going to come to her rescue.

Cutting in as tight an orbit as she could calculate, hoping to use a slingshot maneuver with the gas giant's gravity, the *Curiosity* skimmed the planet's upper atmosphere. Unfortunately, her ionization trail among the highest clouds only gave the black robots an exact route to follow. Her ship vibrated and shook, and the robots kept shooting. Four black craft were behind her now, and she punched down into the layers, hoping to use the thick clouds as a smoke screen, but the relentless pursuers had her locked into their sensors.

As a last-ditch effort, she ejected an ekti canister and detonated it an instant later so the explosion rippled through the clouds, scooping out a void in the mist. She hoped the bugbots would assume her ship had exploded.

As the light and shockwave faded, she deactivated the *Curiosity*'s engines and her emissions, playing possum. The ship drifted under its own momentum, sinking like a stone. Everything was quiet except for the atmosphere buffeting her hull.

Swallowing hard, she patted the capsule in her pocket. "We'll just hang here and stay quiet." She kept her voice to a whisper, though it was ridiculous to think the bugbots might hear her. Thick clouds masked the view from her windowports. Her stomach lurched with panic as the *Curiosity* kept sinking deeper, and she desperately wanted to power up her engines, regain altitude. She would just fall and fall until she reached an equilibrium at some depth, and that wouldn't be a bad thing. She could hang down there for a week and then sneak back out. Alas, the black robots would not be departing anytime soon, and they would detect her as soon as she tried to leave.

She would worry about that later.

Kevin J. Anderson

For fifteen minutes—fifteen long, agonizing minutes—the *Curiosity* simply plummeted. Rlinda could barely breathe, though she was under no acceleration at all. When she saw no sign of the robots, a spark of hope began to flicker inside her heart.

A looming black shape appeared in the clouds in front of her, an angular robot attack vessel cruising through the area. Spotting her, it instantly flared its running lights, powered up its weapons. Rlinda didn't bother to set a course, simply launched her ship forward and plowed away through the clouds.

The robot's blasters ignited fireworks inside the mists, and Rlinda raced up and out of the clouds again, following the curvature of Dhula and careening non-stop through the turbulence. She ricocheted off the high-pressure wall of an atmospheric super-storm, used the deflection to angle upward in a direct trajectory to orbit.

She didn't look back, but the occasional potshots streaking past told her that the robots were still there. Finally, pulling high-rising mists with her, the *Curiosity* shot out of the atmosphere and up into space. She didn't slow, just kept racing toward the scattered moons and debris.

The robots came after her. And she saw more of them ahead, black ships rushing to intercept her.

Rlinda removed one hand from the piloting controls to touch the capsule in her pocket. She'd always imagined—in a sappy and romantic dream—that her ashes and Bebob's would be shot out together into space, mingling among the stars.

As the robots closed in, she realized that might actually happen, though not in the way she had wanted. And much sooner than she had imagined.

CHAPTER TWENTY-SEVEN

Elisa Enturi

Cloud Nine continued to tear itself apart in a cascade of malfunctions. Given a competent engineering crew and adequate resources, any one of the weak links could have been patched up, Elisa supposed ... but her engineer had been sucked out into the clouds, competent or not. She herself was the only competent one left, and she certainly couldn't hold the remaining modules together.

This was a disaster.

The two intact modules shook and vibrated. Some of the seals were breaking open, and she could see they would not last long. Moments after any breach occurred, they would plunge into the clouds.

She had worried about the slim possibility of a hydrogue attack, but she had not worried about flawed materials or workmanship on these well-proven Iswander modules. They should have been perfectly reliable. She couldn't believe Mr. Iswander would tolerate unsafe equipment.

He had warned her as soon as he learned of the flaw, but too late, and she had been unable to fix the problem in time. Now, they were all going to die—she was realistic enough to assume that—and Lee Iswander would be ruined.

If only it had been a real hydrogue attack, then no one would have blamed him for the damage. The deep-core aliens had destroyed numerous helpless structures during the Elemental War.

Anil and Shar ran into the main chamber, flailing their hands. "What should we do? How can we help?"

"Old Bessie," suggested Kipps. "We can climb aboard and ride this out."

"That old wreck won't survive any attack," said Fourth.

Kipps knotted his fists. "I haven't seen any evidence of attack. Where are the warglobes? Where are the blasts? This place is just falling apart. That skybus might keep us alive until the retrieval ship comes in two days."

Elisa knew they might be able to huddle together aboard Old Bessie, and if they were rescued, the survivors would tell everyone how Cloud Nine had simply broken into pieces, that the Iswander modules were unreliable and dangerous—the very modules that had made the company's fortune. A backlash against Iswander Industries would ripple across the Confederation. There would be an uproar.

She couldn't have that.

"I'll see if the bus is still intact." She staggered across the swaying deck over to the external controls. "It may have broken loose."

Tel Robek's scout ship was still anchored on its platform, but Old Bessie had been attached to a lower egress port, where the passengers could climb aboard. She found it, but she had to keep them occupied. "Go to the main chamber, over by the egress hatch." Elisa worked the controls, and before anyone could see what she was doing, she quietly disengaged Old Bessie. The skybus broke away from its anchoring cradle and dropped off, gently spinning away into the winds.

As the skybus disengaged, the survivors felt the sudden lurch in the remaining modules. "What happened? Did we get struck again?" cried Shar.

"I still didn't see any hydrogues out there," said Fourth.

Kipps went to the lower egress hatch. Though it was dark, he could still see the large shape tumbling away. "Bessie just disengaged! The skybus broke free."

The others groaned and wept. "That was our only hope!" Anil said.

Elisa kept busy with her work. "The docking clamp must have been unstable. Everyone remain here—I've got an idea. I need to seal this module. I'll do a separation countdown so that it remains intact."

"And then we're just going to wait here until rescue comes?" Fourth asked.

Without levitation engines, the modules would be crushed within hours, but she didn't tell them that. Elisa downloaded files from the main wallscreen, took the small data crystal with her. "Everyone stay calm. There's still a chance this will all turn out right, but you have to do exactly as I say. Remain together."

Though terrified, they listened to her. They trusted her.

"I'm going to try to make it to my ship," said Robek. "I can fly out, make sure rescue is coming."

But Elisa was well ahead of him, already at the door hatch and moving before anyone realized what she had in mind. "Sadly, rescue isn't coming. But I'll make sure the rest of the Confederation knows about the worst hydrogue attack since the end of the War. These gas giants still aren't safe."

They cried out in confusion. "What are you talking about?" Robek demanded.

The others were completely baffled, Kipps drew himself up, his face flushed with anger. He knew what she was doing. "How dare you—"

She darted through the hatch and sealed it behind her as she cycled through to the black winds. She had already started the separation countdown for the two remaining modules, but she had bypassed the main systems. As soon as the modules disengaged from each other, they would break apart, but Elisa would be far away by that time.

She ran to the sleek Iswander scout ship and climbed aboard, cursing herself for her poor planning. How could she not have established an evacuation routine? Too expensive and too time-consuming. What if there had been an actual hydrogue attack?

She made a mental note to build that into her next test run, if she ever bothered with the sky hotel concept again. Meanwhile, she felt shame and disappointment. She had meant to prove herself to Iswander, to create another innovative business venture to increase his cash streams.

She had to salvage this before she could dream big again—which meant she had to ensure that the only narrative to emerge from the Cloud Nine disaster was hers, the story she would concoct, one that no one alive could contradict.

Now, in Qhardin's night, she was relieved when the cockpit sealed around her. Bursts of angry transmissions immediately came over the comm, Robek yelling, "Don't you dare take my ship! Damn you, come back here."

"To what purpose?" Elisa muttered to herself without bothering to switch on the comm. Only one person could fit aboard the scout ship, and that was her. The other five would have to remain behind anyway.

After activating the scout ship's engines, she disengaged from the landing deck. When she lifted off, she was pleased at how easily it handled, a new model with all the most modern systems. She tapped into the Cloud Nine main controls as her ship headed away. The separation countdown continued.

She heard overlapping voices, shouts and curses. "Come back for us!"

It had been malicious of her to eject Old Bessie. Maybe those people could have drifted in the clouds, and maybe she could have made it to a nearby system fast enough and send rescue. But, oh, the scandal and political damage those survivors could cause. No, this was much better.

When the countdown ended and the two modules disengaged, the walls split open, and the panicked transmissions rose to a crescendo of screams, then fell silent.

Good. She needed her concentration anyway. No one else was here on all of Qhardin, and the debris of the modules would rapidly disperse and sink down to undetectable levels. No one would ever find a scrap.

She raced out into space and set course back to Earth. Robek had the best small-scale Ildiran stardrive and sufficient ekti to take her home. At top speed, the flight would take just under two days, so she would have plenty of time during the flight to complete her preparations.

Elisa had work to do. Streaking out of the Qhardin system on autopilot, she called up the archival images of old hydrogue attacks. The footage had been dramatic and horrifying, the most terrifying eyewitness recordings from the War. She had a wealth of images never before seen by the public. Considering the chaos that would have occurred if the alien warglobes did open fire on the hotel complex, she could make do with what she had. Her own testimony would be convincing.

As the ship flew home, Elisa selected the most horrific archival images and began to cobble together her incident report.

CHAPTER TWENTY-EIGHT

Rlinda Kett

hat good are weapons if you don't use them? Rlinda thought. She charged ahead with nothing left to lose. When she opened fire with her fore and aft jazers, fortunately—and unfortunately—there were so many black robot ships all around her, she couldn't miss. The energy blasts scorched the side of one enemy vessel and struck the engines of another. Her aft jazers took out a third.

The robots responded in kind, hammering the *Curiosity*'s shields. Ionization flares like starbursts appeared around her windowports, and she kept flying, though she knew she couldn't outrun energy weapons. When she had played dead deep under the gas giant clouds, she had maintained radio silence, but now she activated her distress beacon again. No point in hiding.

As she roared pell-mell away from Dhula, her sensors detected an electromagnetic flurry ahead, a buzzing knot of overlapping communications, indecipherable machine language coming from the derelict warliner. Rlinda veered away, not wanting to go anywhere close to that hornet's nest. She had enough trouble eluding the robot ships.

"Where the hell did they come from? And how did the bugbots get so many new vessels?" She had thought all the evil insect machines had been wiped out in the War, but Rlinda's inquisitiveness was diminished as a direct result of being fired upon.

A robot ship flew directly ahead of her, trying to match her speed. "Out of my way, damn you!" She blasted it with her jazers, hammering until the black hull reddened and then broke apart. As the ship exploded in front of her, she flew through the debris storm. Her shields went redline. Flares engulfed her. The ship rocked and rattled, but Rlinda kept roaring forward. She considered whooping wildly and uselessly, but no one would hear her.

That last barrage had just depleted her forward jazers. Her shields were on their last gasp.

The robot ships closed in, powering up their weapons to finish her off. Collision avoidance alarms screamed louder—as if she needed something else to worry about!

Then a huge, unexpected ship swooped in close, going insanely fast as if trying to shake off the remnants of a lightspeed passage. A second, equally huge ship swept in close behind it. An enormous gout of energy vaporized three of the black robot ships and scrambled the others.

Rlinda looked from side to side, astonished. "What the hell?" Not that she was complaining.

Two fully armed Solar Navy warliners cruised into the Dhula system, homing in on Rlinda's distress beacon. The warliners continued to open fire, blasting one robot ship after another.

Up until now, Rlinda had handled herself reasonably well, one trading vessel against those malicious pursuers, but the Ildiran battleships clearly meant business. The warliners did not ask the robots to surrender, nor did they inquire about Rlinda's status. They merely unleashed an overwhelming barrage and vaporized the remaining eight robot ships.

Panting hard, Rlinda watched the dazzling energy bursts fade and the tumbling debris spread in the shockwave clouds. She opened the comm and swallowed twice before she could speak. "Thank you, Ildirans. Next time we're together in a spaceport bar, I will buy every single one of your crew a drink."

Adar Zan'nh's face appeared on her screen. He looked stern and annoyed. "We did not expect to find you here, Captain Kett."

"Sorry, I just wanted to help you find your missing warliner. I didn't expect to find a bugbot infestation. What are they doing out here? Why are there any left at all?"

"In the past, Klikiss robots have hidden themselves and gone into hibernation," Zan'nh said. "Clearly, not all were eradicated in the War." His lips pressed together in a grim line. "We will remedy that here."

As her systems slowly began to recharge and reboot, Rlinda followed the warliner escort back toward the half-dismantled derelict. Black beetle-like figures swarmed by the hundreds over the broken hull, but most of the angular ships had scattered.

"Honest, I didn't mean to intrude," Rlinda explained. "I did intercept Qul Loar'nh's transmissions, and I learned what happened. They had a reactor breach, and the entire crew received a lethal radiation dose. In his last report, Qul Loar'nh asked if their bodies could be taken back to Ildira and incinerated under the seven suns." She shook her head, looking at the partially dismantled skeleton of the ship as the other warliners converged on their target.

"We will incinerate them here," Zan'nh said, "while eradicating the enemy."

The Ildiran warliners opened fire on the infested wreck. Brilliant bursts scored the dead ship's hull, searing dozens of black robots at a time, and the bombardment continued, without pause, turning the drifting warliner to slag.

Rlinda's jazer banks had recharged up to ten percent. Good enough. "Might as well contribute," she said. She opened fire, adding to the barrage for good effect. The weapons didn't stop firing until there was nothing left but a stain of thermal energy.

Adar Zan'nh transmitted, "Thank you, Captain Kett. We have taken care of the problem."

"I hope so," Rlinda said, not convinced. "But why were the robots here at all? What were they doing?"

"The black robots have been destroyed," Zan'nh said. "They cannot possibly have sufficient numbers remaining to pose any further threat."

"I wasn't worried about their numbers, so much as about their schemes," Rlinda said. "I don't trust them."

From his command nucleus, the Adar added a perfunctory, "The Solar Navy will finish operations here and report to the Mage-Imperator. If you will provide me with copies of the transmissions you intercepted, Captain Kett, I trust you have no further business in the Dhula system." His meaning was clear.

"I think I can go home now," she said, "after I patch up a few systems." She took an hour to perform basic repairs to her ship before she dared activate the Ildiran stardrive. She wished she could snoop around here long enough to get some answers.

This couldn't be just a tiny cluster of black robots that had hidden at the end of the Elemental War. They were up to something. The robots were intentionally dismantling the warliner, hauling its materials and components away ... somewhere. To what purpose? What were they up to?

Oddly, the Adar was not bothered by the questions that plagued her, but Ildirans had a completely different mindset from humans. With no other option, she took her questions with her when the battered *Curiosity* flew home.

CHAPTER TWENTY-NINE

Daniel

The spore storm was over, and the people had survived. Most of them. The grieka plants had blossomed and burst, then died, although many of them in the valley had been eradicated by Bjorn and Olaf's tireless efforts with the targeted incinerators, blackening the spores so they would not germinate next time. Thick smoke lingered in the air, making breathing even more difficult. Those who had refused respirator filters for the spores finally relented and used the masks until the smoke and soot settled out of the air.

Daniel helped finish digging the last of the new graves and buried the remaining bodies. Twenty-two neo-Amish dead from the worst of the spore storm, but they would have been joined by hundreds more casualties if he had not gone through the Klikiss transportal and secured help from the Confederation. Jeremiah Huystra would have condemned his decision, but Daniel stood by it. As he held his wife and three children, he had no doubt whatsoever he had made the right decision. He had saved them.

But as he gazed across the burned valley floor, the blackened crops, he felt a lingering fear and sadness. They would be a long time recovering from this.

Olaf looked satisfied with his efforts, though. "Sometimes it takes a strong and determined person to do a hard task, even if the others around you can't see it." He stroked his beard. "Clan Reeves has been in that situation for the past nine years."

Serene looked very worried. "But our crops are all burned. What are we going to eat?"

"Dying from toxic spores or from starvation … it seems a sad choice," Bjorn said.

Serene sighed. "And Father Jeremiah is gone. We've been too weary even to select a new leader."

"We have supplies from previous years," Daniel said. "The neo-Amish always plan for lean times. It'll be thin, but it may be enough. We can explore wider, go hunting, harvest wild plants." He held her tightly. "We'll survive."

"It need not be that hard," said Olaf. "You introduced yourself to King Peter and Queen Estarra. You would be welcome back in the Confederation. Other ships would bring supplies to you. You wouldn't need to starve."

There was a time when Daniel would have jumped at the possibility, but now it made him shudder. "Thank you, but … no. I used to love the outside world and the familiarities of civilization, but not anymore." He shook his head. "The Confederation life isn't for these people. Exposed to outsiders, they would die just as surely as if they had no food. We'll find other ways. We know how to be self-sufficient."

Olaf gave a slow nod. "I respect your choice." Then his lips quirked in a small smile. "Clan Reeves already knows where you live, but I will promise never to return here. Our clan members will forget about Happiness entirely."

Realizing that his answer would determine the future of their settlement, Daniel knew what Father Jeremiah would have wanted. "We're fine here. Some people like to be left alone."

Olaf gave another grim nod. "That, too, I can understand."

☾ • ☽

A week later, on the pretext that he was going out to find wild fruit trees, Daniel climbed the slope to the Klikiss transportal.

The stone trapezoid stood silent and alien, a gateway to countless possibilities.

Behind him, the blackened fields and meadows were already showing a faint blur of green as new shoots rose up, rejuvenated by the fire and fertile ash. Healthy neo-Amish men and women bustled about like worker insects, marking off, tilling, and planting new crops in hopes they could be harvested before the cold dry season set in.

Up in the high meadows, the smaller village was also getting back on its feet. There, they had suffered many more casualties because the sporeflowers had matured sooner, and because the Confederation anti-allergens had come too late to help them. But the whole neo-Amish community pulled together. They helped one another. They grieved together, and they celebrated life together. Once again, Daniel realized how glad he was to be here.

He reached the flat portal that had been erected thousands of years ago by the insect race. Encircling the stone window, coordinate tiles were etched with incomprehensible Klikiss symbols. He didn't know where any of those tiles might lead him, except for the one that had taken him to the planet Auridia. He stared at the designs, pondered the possibilities.

This stone transportal was like an escape hatch, and he always had the chance to change his mind and leave. But he knew in his heart he was satisfied to be here with these people, with his family. He didn't want the next time to be easier, or the next. No matter what, he would never need anything from the outside again.

He stared for a long moment, making sure he had no second thoughts. Before he could begin to doubt himself, he picked up a rock and smashed the control and power unit at the base of the stone trapezoid. Jeremiah Huystra had done a similar thing, but Daniel was more thorough. He kept smashing until the circuitry was thoroughly destroyed. The transportal would never activate again.

When the system lay in ruins, he brushed his hands together. He was home now. *Home*. After adjusting his broad-brimmed hat and scratching the thick beard on his face, Daniel turned about and walked back to his real Happiness.

CHAPTER THIRTY

Elisa Enturi

By the time her scout ship returned to Earth, Elisa had plenty of time to concoct and rehearse her story. After building the framework of what had supposedly happened to the Cloud Nine hotel, she scoured through the database of hydrogue images, altered and manipulated them to fit the details, and she laid out her story.

The hydrogues had not been seen in nine years, and they were believed to be huddled deep inside their gas giants. Elisa had voluntarily taken the risk—as had her four guests, along with the Iswander employees who had volunteered for the job. High risk, high reward. Lee Iswander certainly understood that, as did all Roamers, and many ambitious Roamer operations had failed disastrously as well. No one could fault Elisa—and by extension, Iswander—for pushing the envelope like this.

But she had to make it sound plausible.

Kipps, Candeen, Juvia, and Fourth had all signed iron-clad waivers; Tel Robek, Oni Delkin, Shar, and Anil were covered by similar Iswander employment documents. When coming out to Qhardin, they all acknowledged the risks of a possible hydrogue attack, but even Elisa had dismissed the idea. Surely, even if the deep-core aliens came back, they would target much larger operations, such as the skymines run by clan Duquesne on Belliros. Why would they bother with a tiny cluster of modules?

She would have to make her shock convincing, make sure everyone believed her that the hydrogues were the culprits.

Elisa pulled together and manipulated the archival images— parting cloud banks, the murky crystalline sphere of a spiked hydrogue warglobe with dancing blue lightning that arced out and struck. More warglobes, more attacks … screams and detonations … module walls collapsing. The images were unsteady, blurred, broken up through chaos and power surges.

She thought they were extremely persuasive.

Reaching the Earth system, she considered racing in on a pell-mell course with emergency signals squawking, but she decided that would seem too forced. Besides, that wasn't Elisa Enturi's personality. Her journey home from Qhardin had taken nearly two days, so why would she still be frantic with terror? She could pretend to be in shock, grieving and frightened, but no one would believe a continued state of mindless panic after all that time … and certainly not from a woman like her. Given all that time to think, Elisa concluded that she should report the tragedy to Lee Iswander, who would take the matter to the authorities.

Her hardest decision, as she flew in toward Earth, was whether to tell Iswander what had really happened. She abhorred the idea of lying to him, or even just hiding the truth. She worried that he would object to her decision, that he would criticize her for the choices she had made, even though she knew she had chosen the right path. The cost of truth was far too high for Iswander Industries, and Elisa wouldn't let her mentor pay it.

No, she would tell him the false story as well, make him believe that the malicious hydrogues had destroyed her test hotel. Iswander would believe her because *she* never lied to him. And it would give him plausible deniability.

She landed the scout ship on the upper deck of the headquarters building and immediately went to see him. Iswander made time for her right away. As she stepped into the office, she composed her expression, made sure she looked sufficiently stricken, but professional. "Sir, my test-run sky hotel on Qhardin was … a disaster."

He looked alarmed. "Did you get my warning? The modules were unsafe."

"It wasn't the modules, sir. Shortly after your scout arrived with the recorded message, we saw turbulence in the clouds, something rising from deep below. Hydrogues attacked us. They destroyed everything." With her mouth set in a grim line, she extended the datapack across the desk, plugged it in to a player, and projected the sequence of carefully edited images.

Iswander watched with widening eyes and a cold expression. "We thought the gas giants were safe."

Elisa nodded. "I'm sorry, sir. As soon as I received your warning, I would have decommissioned the modules and withdrawn the initial guests until we could make repairs. But I never had the chance." She swallowed hard. "The hydrogues were merciless."

He leaned back in the chair, turning pale. "We'll have to report this. Gas giants are still dangerous." He placed his hands on the desktop and curled his fingers into fists. "Stardrive fuel is incredibly expensive, and the Roamer operations were just beginning to supply ekti again. They thought the hydrogues wouldn't harass their operations, but once we release this …" He drew a deep breath and shook his head. "This will drive many of them away again. They'll be too afraid."

"You once told me that Roamers aren't afraid of danger. They weigh the risks and make their choice."

"This will change the parameters of their decisions. Some of the Roamers might delay implementation of their new skymines. Oh, the consequences!" He replayed the horrific images again, visibly wincing as the warglobes lanced out with deadly lightning bolts. "I'm glad you got away." He looked at her. "And there were no other survivors? No chance they're still alive?"

She squared her shoulders. "No, sir. No witnesses."

He raised his eyebrows, but didn't ask what she meant. Perhaps he suspected, but didn't want to know.

"Once we make this announcement, there will be an uproar across the Confederation. Military forces will launch for Qhardin and investigate."

"They won't find anything, sir," Elisa said. "Everything's been destroyed, sunk far into the clouds." She couldn't tell if he looked relieved.

He leaned forward on his desk. "For now, we should table your idea of creating sky hotel complexes. Do you agree, Ms. Enturi?"

"Yes, sir, I agree. Let me know if there's anything I can do to help. Iswander Industries will weather this. It wasn't our fault. A tragedy."

He nodded distractedly. "Yes, but perhaps we should look for other opportunities ... on planets where we don't need to worry about hydrogues.

☾ • ☽

When she went to relax in her usual bar, Elisa did not expect to encounter Garrison Reeves. Once they retrieved the spare modules after the shameful quarrel with his stubborn father, she had not expected to see the young man ever again, and she certainly had no interest in the backward activities of clan Reeves.

But Garrison came over, grinning and hopeful. "I've been coming here for three days, hoping to see you. Apparently, you're not a regular in this place?"

She sat back and regarded him with a cool expression. "I've been on another mission."

He took a seat next to her. "Oh, where?"

"An obscure gas giant, Qhardin. You wouldn't have heard of it."

"Qhardin?" Garrison smiled. "Roamers once did skymining there, but the cloud harvesters were abandoned when the drogues delivered their ultimatum."

Lacing her fingers together, she gave him a hard look. "The hydrogues haven't entirely given up on the planet."

To his widening eyes, she told him the story—her concocted story. He was astonished, but clearly believed everything she said. Elisa relaxed, knowing it would get easier to tell the story each time.

She changed the subject. "Why did you come back here? I thought you'd be trapped at Rendezvous, sent to your room because of your misbehavior."

He snorted. "I left there for good after we rounded up the modules. My father has no more hold on me. I won't give up my life to stay trapped in the past. I have too many ideas, too many ambitions." He lowered his voice. "I think you and I have a lot in common. Maybe we can work together."

She considered the idea. He wasn't wrong. Though he'd been raised in an archaic Roamer clan, Garrison did want to lift himself up and make a mark on the future.

The server came by with two glasses of Elisa's chosen wine, and Garrison at least pretended to like it. He picked up his glass, and she raised hers as she nodded slowly. "We might be able to match our ambitions. There are certainly worse partners I can imagine." She smiled at him. "Yes, we may have a great future together."

CHAPTER THIRTY-ONE

Olaf Reeves

After leaving Happiness, Olaf was troubled. "I sympathize with those people who just want to be isolated, with no interference from Confederation politics," he told Bjorn. "I can certainly understand that. But I feel they might have a hard time ahead."

Bjorn agreed. "The prospect of losing a third of their population every ten years ... and they didn't have many people to start with. This time, fortunately, we brought the tools to save them, and the filters and facemasks will help them survive the next time."

"*If* they use them," Olaf said. "I'm not entirely sure they will." He couldn't guess how much backlash Daniel would face for breaking their strict rules. But Olaf would honor their request and not come back. That was their decision. "I can't force them to use the tools ... any more than the other clans can force us to give up our dream of rebuilding Rendezvous."

Yes, Olaf Reeves understood the neo-Amish all too well.

Olaf stroked his beard. "In fact, we'll alter our own records back at Rendezvous to make sure no one thinks to go back there. It's a matter of honor."

"What if they need help again?" Bjorn asked.

"Then they will have to help themselves. It may sound harsh, but that is what they want. Survival is a gift and an accomplishment, not a miracle. It happens through our own efforts. The neo-Amish know how to take care of themselves, as do we. We have our Guiding Star, and clan Reeves knows where it shines." He lowered his voice. "Most of us do, at least."

Bjorn looked over with a commiserating expression. "Garrison will be back. He's your son. He's the future clan leader. He has to come back."

"Garrison gave up his Roamer blood as surely as if he opened his veins and spilled it out onto the deck plates. Dale is my only son now, and he needs to be trained. We must make sure he's properly oriented and will follow the right Guiding Star." He lifted his eyebrows as a thought struck him. "In fact, let's make sure Dale marries Sendra Detemer, and soon. She has enough backbone of her own to keep his spine straight."

Bjorn chuckled. "Sendra? She certainly has her own opinions."

"She has confidence, as well as competence. She'll be a good Roamer wife. And so long as she believes in the proper future of Rendezvous, then we will all be on the same page."

Olaf knew that Rendezvous would continue to regrow, one small step at a time, exactly according to its original design. He remained disappointed at how King Peter and Queen Estarra had dismissed him. Once again clan Reeves was on their own. They were always on their own, but they survived, and they achieved what was necessary.

Bjorn took an alternate route back from Happiness, and out in the far fringe of a solar system en route, he picked up an anomaly on the scanners, enough to make him curious. "Look at this, Olaf." He pointed to the glitch on the screen. "Too small to be an asteroid but it seems irregular. An artificial construction. Something large. maybe five times as big as Newstation."

Olaf disengaged the Ildiran stardrive and dropped them out of lightspeed. "Sounds like someone was even more ambitious than the Roamers were. Better have a look."

Bjorn piloted them closer to the object ahead. The system's sun was so far away it was only a bright star, leaving them in the outer darkness. "If it's a space station, why would anyone build it all the way out here? What possible strategic or commercial use could it have? It's on the fringe of a system, and the system itself doesn't have any useful planets, just an asteroid belt."

"Somebody considered it important. Or maybe they're hiding. Are you sure it's not on any of the old Hansa maps? Or even the Ildiran star charts?"

Bjorn double checked. "Nothing, Olaf. No record of anyone having an interest in this system at all."

Ahead, the structure began to take shape on their screens. It was huge, and angular, obviously artificial. The darkness around them was spattered with a faint panoply of stars. "It wouldn't be Ildiran. Their race is afraid of the dark, and they'd never build something this far from a sun."

Bjorn said, "I doubt the Hansa could have constructed something this big without leaving records."

Olaf completed more scans. "No energy signature. No thermal emissions, no power traces. It's reached a balance of ambient temperature. Nobody's home, and nobody's been home for a long time."

They illuminated their running lights and sent out active sensor pings, building up a detailed image. Bjorn stared at the looming construction and said with clear awe in his voice, "No human built that."

"No," Olaf said, "I don't think so."

The derelict station was the size of a city, built like a huge metal snowflake with five angled arms extending at misaligned axes from a central hub. Each axis was studded with geometrical modules, huge habitation complexes, incomprehensible structures.

"It's a dead, empty city," Olaf said.

"Do you think the Klikiss might have built it?" Bjorn asked.

Frowning, Olaf shook his head as their ship circled the derelict structure. "You've seen their termite-mound cities and their swarmships. Nothing about this thing looks Klikiss."

Bjorn seemed fascinated. "We can take a succession of images and deliver a report to the Confederation. Plenty of people will want to salvage it, but we logged the discovery first."

Olaf felt uneasy. "It's clear that whoever constructed this intended to remain hidden. The builders didn't want to call attention to themselves, and they must have had a damn good reason."

He couldn't stop thinking of Daniel and the neo-Amish, how they clung to their isolation as their home, despite the hardships, wanting no help or interference.

Olaf made up his mind. "Whoever these mysterious builders were, I'm sure they didn't want this great city to become a tourist attraction. We'll mark it for ourselves, but ..." He tapped his fingers on the deck, thinking of his own clan, of Rendezvous, of Garrison. "It's not our place to intrude. They wanted to be left alone, so we will leave them."

He activated the engines and plotted a course forward. "Log it as your own discovery, Bjorn, but we won't call attention to this derelict city, any more than we'll send curiosity seekers to Happiness."

The other man sounded surprised and disappointed. "But there's much we can learn here. Who knows what it might contain?"

"Indeed, who knows? But it's out here in the dark, and my Guiding Star doesn't point to it. This place doesn't concern us. The builders wanted to be left alone, and we will respect that." He activated the stardrive, and the ship streaked away from the dark alien city. "It'll be our secret. Someday we may need to go back, but right now we have to rebuild Rendezvous. That is our only goal."

CHAPTER THIRTY-TWO

Rlinda Kett

By the time Rlinda returned to Kett Shipping Headquarters, Tasia Tamblyn and Robb Brindle had found their own way back home from Newstation. They had spent the intervening days catching up on admin work in her penthouse offices.

Robb had occupied the big trader woman's desk while she was gone, and now he reluctantly relinquished the seat. "Your operations are a mess, Rlinda."

"I tried to organize your ship schedules," Tasia said. "Kett Shipping has some redundant routes, while a bunch of distant systems aren't being served at all. We need a better balance."

Rlinda was eager to tell her story of finding the infestation of black robots. "I've been a little busy. You might have noticed some damage to the *Curiosity*'s hull?"

Robb looked up in alarm. "Damage? What happened? Are you all right?"

"Is the ship all right?" Tasia said.

Rlinda made a raspberry sound in her direction. "Thank you for your concern. We had a little incident with black robots in the Ildiran Empire." While Tasia and Robb demanded explanations,

Rlinda strung them along. "Such a tale should be told only over a nice meal. If you'll help me prepare it …?"

She had a full kitchen in her offices for private use, and she decided she had an appetite for chicken piccata. So she pounded out the chicken breasts, dredged them in flour, and began to fry them in a hot pan as she told them about delivering the treelings to the Mage-Imperator, tracking down the missing Solar Navy warliner, and finding the swarm of Klikiss robots tearing it to pieces.

"I wasn't looking for that much excitement. I thought it was fun to be Trade Minister, flitting from system to system and doing my business—and I was damned good at it." She set the golden chicken fillets aside as the pasta finished boiling, which she then dumped in a colander to drain. She added the capers, the lemons, and used her finger to taste the sauce. "But somehow, those duties are no longer quite so satisfying. I've made my mark. Time to retire."

She scooped up pasta onto three plates, dividing the portions equally. Robb and Tasia watched, fascinated with her story, but also clearly hungry from the smells of her cooking.

"I promised Peter and Estarra that I would serve as Trade Minister during the formative days of the Confederation. They needed someone they could trust, and they wanted me to help build stability, but nine years is enough for that. I have other business." With tongs, she placed a fried fillet on each nest of pasta, then ladled over the lemon sauce with capers. "It's time for them to find a replacement."

Tasia nodded. "Good call. Kett Shipping is a booming business. You should devote your efforts here." She gestured behind her to the illuminated screens on Rlinda's desk, the trade routes, the ships in transit, her contract pilots, the database of cargoes being delivered, items requested from specific markets across the Spiral Arm. "And as we've seen, running it is a full-time job."

"Indeed it is," Rlinda said. "More than a full-time job. In fact, it takes two people." She handed Robb and Tasia each their plates. "Two people such as yourselves."

She waited for them to understand what she was saying. "Tasia Tamblyn and Robb Brindle, I choose you as my acting administrators of Kett Shipping. You'll handle all the nonsense, arrange the flights, deal with whiny captains, build up my profits, untangle the red tape." She huffed. "In fact, I'll even let you use the *Voracious Curiosity*—except when I need it of course."

Robb blinked. "Thank you, Rlinda! That's amazing."

"Sounds like a lot of work," Tasia said. "Do we get a raise?"

"How about profit sharing?" Rlinda said.

"Works for me."

Rlinda garnished her plate with parsley, then reached over to drop a sprig of green on the other two plates. "Have to do it right." She led them in to a small table in her office, where they sat to eat. She cut into her piccata and savored the first taste, letting the chicken melt in her mouth along with the citrus tang of the lemon, the piquant pungency of the capers. "Perfect."

Tasia and Robb each wolfed down their portions. "This is why I like taking meetings with Rlinda," Tasia said.

Robb added, "I don't particularly enjoy meetings otherwise."

"If you're going to be my acting administrators, you better learn to enjoy meetings, with or without food," Rlinda said.

In between mouthfuls, Tasia wiped her lips with a napkin. "What about you, Rlinda? If you give up being Trade Minister and you hand over Kett Shipping, what will you do? You're not exactly ... sedentary."

Rlinda let out a laugh that almost made her choke on her pasta. "Sedentary? Do I look like a slim athlete?"

"Slim or not, you're always busy," Robb said. "You aren't the type to sit on a beach and read a book."

Rlinda closed her eyes and sighed, imagining the picture, maybe with BeBob.... She opened her eyes. "You're right, but I want to do what I enjoy most. I have three restaurants, one here, one on Relleker, one on Theroc. That's where I'd rather spend my time instead of being fired upon by black robots."

"I see your point," Robb said.

Tasia finished her chicken and scooped up a forkful of pasta. "Spreading food like this across the Spiral Arm might be the best way to keep peace among the races."

Rlinda smiled at the compliment. "And you haven't even tasted dessert yet."

ABOUT THE AUTHOR

Kevin J. Anderson has published 140 books, 54 of which have been national or international bestsellers. He has written numerous novels in the Star Wars, X-Files, Dune, and DC Comics universes, as well as unique steampunk fantasy novels *Clockwork Angels* and *Clockwork Lives*, written with legendary rock drummer Neil Peart, based on the concept album by the band Rush. His original works include the Saga of Seven Suns series, the Terra Incognita fantasy trilogy, the Saga of Shadows trilogy, and his humorous horror series featuring Dan Shamble, Zombie PI. He has edited numerous anthologies, written comics and games, and the lyrics to two rock CDs. Anderson and his wife Rebecca Moesta are the publishers of WordFire Press.

IF YOU LIKED ...

If you liked *Whistling Past the Graveyard*,
you might also enjoy:

Veiled Alliances
Blindfold
Hopscotch

OTHER WORDFIRE PRESS TITLES
BY KEVIN J. ANDERSON

Alien Landscapes #1
Alien Landscapes #2
Alternitech
Artifact
Blindfold
Climbing Olympus
Clockwork Angels: The Comic Scripts
Comrades in Arms

Dan Shamble, Zombie PI Series
Dan Shamble 1: Death Warmed Over
Dan Shamble 2: Unnatural Acts
Dan Shamble 3: Hair Raising
Dan Shamble 4: Slimy Underbelly
Working Stiff

Dark Labyrinth #1
Dark Labyrinth #2
Drilling Deep
Fantastic Realms #1
Fantastic Realms #2

Fondest of Memories
Frog Kiss

Gamearth Series
Gamearth 1:Gamearth
Gamearth 2: Gameplay
Gamearth 3: Game's End

Hopscotch
Job Qualifications

Million Dollar Series
Million Dollar Productivity
Million Dollar Professionalism for the Writer
Worldbuilding: From Small Towns to Entire Universes

Redmond's Private Screening
Resurrection, Inc.
The Saga of Seven Suns: Veiled Alliances

By Kevin J Anderson & Doug Beason
Assemblers of Infinity
Craig Kreident #1: Virtual Destruction
Craig Kreident #2: Fallout
Craig Kreident #3: Lethal Exposure
Ignition

Ill Wind
Lifeline
Magnetic Reflections
Prisons
The Trinity Paradox

By Kevin J Anderson & Rebecca Moesta
Collaborators
Crystal Doors #1: Island Realm
Crystal Doors #2: Ocean Realm
Crystal Doors #3: Sky Realm

The Star Challengers Series
Star Challengers #1: Moonbase Crisis
Star Challengers #2: Space Station Crisis
Star Challengers #3: Asteroid Crisis

Kevin J. Anderson & Neil Peart
Clockwork Angels
Clockwork Lives
Drumbeats

Our list of other WordFire Press authors and titles is always growing. To find out more and to see our selection of titles, visit us at:

wordfirepress.com